Sadie isn't trying to take advantage of you.

She was here at his castle with an ulterior motive, though.

Yeah, to help you.

Enzo didn't want help. He didn't want company. He didn't want a party. He didn't want cheering up. He didn't want his solitude disturbed.

He wanted to be left alone to recover his strength, to process all that had happened, to solder the broken bits of himself back together.

What he didn't want was sparkling eyes, glossy hair and lips so pretty they made him wonder what it would be like to kiss them. *Again.* Long-term romance might now be barred from his future, but he had no problem with fleeting hook ups. And he'd never forgotten the kiss he and Sadie had shared all of those years ago.

He shook himself. What he did have a problem with, though, was hooking up fleetingly with his stepsister's best friend. *That* had the potential to lead to trouble.

Dear Reader,

A grumpy-sunshine, *Beauty and the Beast* story is one of my favorites. The good-hearted fun of the former coupled with the inbuilt angst of the latter gives me all the feels I want in a romance, all the highs and lows that make me happy sigh by the time I reach the last page.

Sadie and Enzo have known each other for a long time. As his stepsister's best friend, though, Sadie has always been off-limits. Which suits Enzo fine! All he wants is to be left alone to recover from his recent car accident. Sadie had the hugest crush on Enzo at the age of fourteen...fifteen...all the way through to eighteen. She's a grown up now, though, and is over such nonsense. Or is she? She can't help finding Enzo, even scarred as he is, magnetically attractive. But he's out of her league and always has been. To fall for him again now would be a disaster, wouldn't it?

It was a joy to watch these two find their way back to one another. I hope it has you happy sighing by the end of the last page, too.

Hugs,

Michelle

FORBIDDEN CINDERELLA IN HIS CASTELLO

MICHELLE DOUGLAS

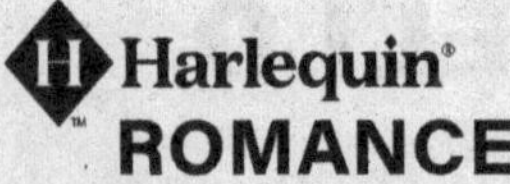

ISBN-13: 978-1-335-47072-0

Recycling programs for this product may not exist in your area.

Forbidden Cinderella in His Castello

For questions and comments about the quality of this book, please contact us at CustomerService@Harlequin.com.

Harlequin Enterprises ULC
22 Adelaide St. West, 41st Floor
Toronto, Ontario M5H 4E3, Canada
www.Harlequin.com

HarperCollins Publishers
Macken House, 39/40 Mayor Street Upper,
Dublin 1, D01 C9W8, Ireland
www.HarperCollins.com

Printed in U.S.A.

Michelle Douglas has been writing for Harlequin since 2007 and believes she has the best job in the world. She lives in a leafy suburb of Newcastle, on Australia's east coast, with her own romantic hero, a house full of dust and books, and an eclectic collection of '60s and '70s vinyl. She loves to hear from readers and can be contacted via her website, michelle-douglas.com.

Books by Michelle Douglas

Harlequin Romance

One Summer in Italy

Unbuttoning the Tuscan Tycoon
Cinderella's Secret Fling

One Year to Wed

Claiming His Billion-Dollar Bride

Summer Escapes

The Venice Reunion Arrangement

Wedding Date in Malaysia
Reclusive Millionaire's Mistletoe Miracle
Waking Up Married to the Billionaire
Tempted by Her Greek Island Bodyguard
Secret Fling with the Billionaire
Tempted by Her Best Friend Billionaire

Visit the Author Profile page at Harlequin.com for more titles.

To Mum, who continues to read my stories
with the same gratifying enthusiasm she always has.
I love you too!

CHAPTER ONE

SADIE STARED OUT of the window as the car wound up the side of the hill towards Enzo's castle. Every now and again she'd catch a glimpse of it: *gobsmacking*. Apparently the view of the castle from the water was extraordinary. However, as she was an average everyday Cinderella and not some society princess with a private yacht, Sadie wasn't going to be fortunate enough to see it from its 'best side'. Not that she was here for the scenery. She was here for the attics.

The thought made her dance in her seat. *You're here for the attics* amongst *other things.*

She did her best to rein in her excitement. She couldn't get too carried away with the attics. Her first priority was Enzo. She was here for him. She'd promised Chelsea.

She grimaced. It was nine years since she'd spent any quality time with him, though. When she'd pointed that out, Chelsea had said, 'But the two of you were always on the same wavelength.'

That was not how Sadie remembered it. She'd *thought* they'd been on the same wavelength.

But…she'd been wrong. It had devastated her at the time, but she'd survived. At eighteen, she'd thought herself such a grown-up, but she'd been nothing more than a child.

Oh, God, what if things were…awkward? She scrubbed a hand over her face. *Stick to the plan.*

Pulling in a breath, she did what she could to slow the racing of her heart. Good advice; she'd stick to the plan. She would not start obsessing over Enzo like some starstruck teenager. She would keep the past firmly in the past. *And* she'd be cheerful.

Besides, it wasn't as if she hadn't seen Enzo at all in the last few years. There'd been Chelsea's wedding. Nothing untoward had happened then. She hadn't immediately started crushing on him. She hadn't followed him with her eyes all evening. She hadn't started wishing and hoping.

Because, after one obligatory 'How are you?', 'Great! How about you?' conversation, you studiously and strenuously avoided him.

Scrunching up her face, she again glared out of the window. All of that stuff was ancient history. She was an adult now and she would behave like an adult. Enzo was going through a challenging time and she'd do whatever she could to help. That was all. Because Chelsea had asked it of her. And she'd do anything for her best friend—her *pregnant* best friend. The fact it had also provided her with the perfect escape from Australia was neither here nor there.

A familiar wave of heaviness settled over her at the reminder of what she'd left behind in Melbourne. Her mother was home. Verity Beckett was back, twenty-seven years after dumping Sadie with her grandparents and heading out into the wide blue yonder, never contacting them again.

Until now. The thing she'd always hoped for as a child had finally happened. But, instead of the bright-eyed, smiling woman she'd secretly imagined, swooping in with big hugs and lots of laughter, Sadie been confronted with a hard-eyed woman with a calculating smile.

What a mess!

No brooding. It was what it was. Time to focus on the future.

Squaring her shoulders, she lifted her chin. She was on an adventure. She was embarking on the first step in her new life away from Australia and her family. That was the Mediterranean Sea down there. She was on the Italian Riviera—*her*—and she wasn't going to let anything spoil this holiday. And, as an expert in repairing antique toys, she was going to enjoy mending a few from the castle for Chelsea and her unborn baby.

Shaking her head, she huffed out a laugh. With everything that was happening in her life, she wasn't going to have time to crush on Enzo. She'd be too busy spending her spare time working on the toys, applying for jobs and planning this new life of hers.

A moment later, she gave another excited shimmy. While they might not be the only reason she was here, those attics were still more than a cover story—she *would* get a chance to explore them. Which meant, amid all the jollying and cheering up she'd promised to do for the unsuspecting Enzo, she'd also get to go treasure-hunting.

A view of the water below emerged as the trees thinned. Still and blue on the late-afternoon air, it looked like something from a travel brochure. Craning her neck, she tried to keep it in view as long as she could. Chelsea had told her the beauty of the Ligurian coast would knock her sideways. Maybe it wouldn't be so hard to drag herself away from the attics after all.

The road curved and the view disappeared. Forest rose up all around them—a forest full of dark pines, like something from a fairy tale. Like the wood Hansel and Gretel had found themselves lost in. Or where the Beast had his castle in *Beauty and the Beast*.

That reference had her wincing. Enzo might be scarred after his accident, but it didn't mean he'd become a growly, snarly beast, despite what Chelsea said. A grump, perhaps, but not a beast.

She pressed her hands together. If he was grumpy, then she'd be the opposite. She'd be bright, breezy and enthusiastic—a breath of fresh air. She'd be the perfect epitome of some guy's little sister's best friend: bright and bubbly, familiar and uncomplicated. Chelsea and Enzo might only be step-siblings—Chelsea's father had married Enzo's mother when Chelsea had been fourteen and Enzo eighteen—but they adored one another. Chelsea called him 'the brother of her heart'. And Chelsea was the sister of Sadie's heart.

Wrought-iron gates in an imposing fence of grey stone swung open, and Enzo's castle came into view. She craned her neck to try and take it all in. When Chelsea had told her it was a small castle, she hadn't realised a small castle wasn't literally *small.* Nor had she envisioned how imposing or beautiful it would be, with its stone walls rising from a paved courtyard to soar into the gentle early-evening sky.

Guido, the driver, directed her to huge double doors, then he and the car disappeared round the side of the house…*uh, castle*. The doors were flung open before Sadie could reach them and a woman Sadie would put in her early fifties beamed at her.

'You must be Miss Sadie Beckett. I'm Luisa Belotti, Signor Lorenzo's housekeeper. Signora Chelsea, she has told me all of your favourite things to eat and I am looking forward to…how do you say it…cooking up a storm?'

Sadie couldn't help but laugh at the warmth of the welcome. 'I'm pleased to meet you, Signora Belotti. I fear I'm going to be totally spoiled for the next fortnight.'

'You must call me Luisa.' Luisa led her inside. 'We want you to feel at home while you are here. It will be nice to have another person to fuss over.'

'Then you must call me Sadie. I…'

She came to a dead halt in the entrance hall, an enormous, whopping room that was all stone and dark wood, with a fireplace that could seat half a dozen people inside of it. How on earth did one feel *at home* in this?

The housekeeper smiled. 'It is impressive, *vero*?'

'Just…wow.'

'Now, would you like to go up to your room to freshen up or would you prefer to see Signor Lorenzo first?'

'Enzo,' she said promptly.

'Excellent. That will give Guido time to take your bags up to your room. And you must be eager to see Signor Lorenzo. I understand it has been quite some time.'

'Ages and ages.'

As she followed Luisa up an impressive set of stairs, Sadie's stomach tightened. She ticked off all the things she knew about Enzo these days: his property developing company was one of the most successful in all of Italy, making him wealthy beyond anyone's wildest dreams; he dated cruel women, if the scathing critiques Chelsea treated her to were anything to go by; and five months ago he and his latest girlfriend had been badly injured in a dreadful car accident.

She pressed her hands together. She had no reason to be nervous. Enzo might've retreated from the world over the course of the last few months, but, considering all that had happened, that was understandable. She didn't doubt he'd host her warmly enough. She was his little sister's best friend. They had *history*. And, luckily, she was no longer the starry-eyed girl she'd once been.

Luisa led her through several large reception rooms to a magnificent drawing room. Light poured in at the wall of windows that arced in a graceful curve to form a grand version of a bay window.

Sadie came to a dead halt again. 'No way! You *have* to be joking me!'

Sadie's feet automatically took her across to that bay of windows to drink in the view with a greedy gaze. A manicured lawn and a strategically wild garden gave way to a view of the Mediterranean that currently reflected the colours of the twilit sky—all soft blues, pinks and silvers. In the still air, it looked as smooth as a mirror.

'No joke.'

The familiar voice had her stomach clenching, but she resisted the urge to swing round. Staring at the view, she smiled.

Enzo used to tease her about her obsession with *Pride and Prejudice*. Would he remember?

'Tell me the truth. When did you first know that you'd fallen in love with Mr Darcy?'

She changed voices. 'I believe I first mistook it from seeing his beautiful grounds at Pemberley.'

'You know that isn't a direct quote?'

'Don't be pedantic. I'm paraphrasing.' Swinging round, she determinedly kept a smile in place and moved across to where he stood in the shadows—tall and solitary, his hands resting on a cane. Luisa quietly retreated out of the room.

Before Sadie could reach him, though, he adjusted the walking stick in such a way as to prevent her from reaching across and hugging him or giving him a peck on the cheek. She fought to keep her eyebrows from shooting up. Instead, she thrust her hand at him, forcing contact. 'Hello, Enzo.'

He had to move the stick from his right hand to his left. Scowling, he shook her hand—a perfunctory single pump practically over before it had begun—but she kept hold of it and moved in a step closer to stare up into his face.

A jagged scar zigzagged across his forehead from his hairline to bisect his left eyebrow. Her stomach clenched up tighter than a lid on a pickle jar. He'd been lucky not to lose an eye! A succession of scars peppered his left cheek. She felt as if her heartbeat were being pressed under glass. 'Hellfire and brimstone,' she murmured, releasing his hand.

Only this time it was he who held her hand captive and refused to let it go. Dark eyes flashed. 'Pretty, isn't it?'

She glowered back. 'Damn it, Enzo, but yes! How can your scars make you look even more beautiful? How is that even possible?'

Her hand was abruptly released and she had to set her legs to stop from falling. He moved the cane back into his right hand, becoming scarily aloof again. 'Stop being ridiculous.'

'I'm not.' And she wasn't. 'A mere mortal like me can only gaze in awe and envy. Mind you, if I had to go through a horrific car accident to win such beauty, I'd give it a hard pass. I'm truly sorry about your accident, Enzo.'

His glare didn't abate. 'Do you know how truly grating your "cheerful" Aussie accent is?'

'I absolutely do,' she said, amping up the cheer factor another notch. Chelsea hadn't been exaggerating when she'd said he'd turned into a grump. If he'd ever spoken to her like that back when she'd been a lovestruck teenager, she'd have died. 'When Chelsea said you'd become bad-tempered, I didn't believe her. I told her you'd always been kindness personified.'

If possible, his scowl deepened. 'You should've believed her.'

'Clearly, but it's going to take more than a bad temper to scare me away.'

He'd started to turn, but he swung back, his frown deepening. 'Why?'

'I have one word for you.' She pointed ceilingward. 'Attics!'

He rolled his eyes.

She sent him the cheeriest of cheerful smiles. 'That, and the fact I'm no longer madly in love with you.'

He nearly dropped his cane. She grinned. In fact, she grinned so hard he ought to be blinded.

Scowling, he led her into an adjacent room—away from the windows with their amazing view, away from the pretty marble fireplace and all the beautiful things. Trailing behind him, she silently pointed to the windows and all the things. *What was wrong with sitting in there?* But he didn't turn round; didn't see her unspoken questions.

This new room was smaller and darker, but that didn't mean it was actually small. Despite the fact it had vaulted ceilings and a fireplace, it lacked the character of the drawing room. It lacked warmth. It lacked…charm.

Was this where he liked to sit? No wonder he'd grown so grumpy and gloomy. She made a silent note to hunt out some colourful cushions and throw rugs to quietly brighten it up. What the room did have, though, was a big-screen TV and a bookcase full of DVDs, which gave her an idea.

He gestured for her to take a seat on the sofa as Luisa returned with a tray of coffee and *petits fours*. 'To tide you over until dinner time,' she said with a smile in Sadie's direction, before promptly departing.

'Chelsea told me you'd be obsessed with the attics.'

She poured him a coffee and handed it across. He sat in a big battered armchair that somehow suited him. She selected a pastry with care. 'She made me promise not to hole myself up there for the entire fortnight.'

His lips twisted, though she didn't understand why. She bit into the pastry—oh, god, it was so good—before gesturing in the direction of the view and the sea. 'With that right on the doorstep, I suspect my promise won't be as hard to keep as I thought it might be.'

A sceptical eyebrow rose, and again she didn't understand what he had to be sceptical about. Actually, it was more than scepticism… Cynicism, perhaps? 'So today you get me on my best behaviour where I don't pester you to immediately show me the attics. That happens tomorrow.' It took a force of will to keep her voice steady and upbeat. 'And speaking of manners…' She set down her coffee and pastry. 'Thank you for having me here, Enzo.'

'I was under the impression I didn't have a choice.'

She stared into those dark, dangerous eyes and frowned—while a wholly disassociated part of her marvelled at the breath of his shoulders. She might've had the biggest crush known to man on Enzo years ago, but she'd never properly *appreciated* those shoulders.

'Look, I know that Chelsea can be…persuasive in her persistence, but—'

'Let's cut the pretence, Sadie.'

What pretence?

'I know my family have sent you to report back on my health, my state of mind and my future plans.'

Just like that, his cynicism made a horrible kind of sense. She could see all too clearly why he really thought she was here. It was lucky she no longer had those stars in her eyes, because they'd have taken a nosedive into the depths of a cold, dark sea right about now.

'You *know* that?' She feigned shock. 'Then I guess you also know, besides sending a detailed report back to your family, I've been instructed to cheer you up and take your mind off your troubles. And, as Chelsea and I thought you'd probably outgrown kites and skateboards, we figured me seducing you might do the trick.'

Because he thought *that* was what she was here for—to seduce him when he was in a weakened state and his defences were down. Did he honestly think Sadie had no pride? A hard ball of something fiery and fierce settled in the pit of her stomach. 'But why stop there, we said, chortling up our sleeves. Why not seduce you into marriage and then I could have the honour of looking after you forever, because…well…looking after a grumpy, entitled man has always been my *one true dream*.'

Best of all, she delivered it with the biggest of cheery smiles.

* * *

Sadie drew out the words 'one true dream' with a mockery that stung. Enzo closed his eyes and pinched the bridge of his nose. Heat prickled his face, his neck, his ears. His skin might be naturally olive, but he doubted it hid the way he flushed.

Not that he deserved the comfort of hiding his embarrassment or shame. Sadie hadn't deserved the bitterness he'd flung at her. Neither did his family. Why couldn't they just leave him alone, though? Why did they have to disturb his peace and solitude?

An invisible eyebrow rose inside him. *Peace?* Okay, fine, just solitude, then. He didn't want anyone disturbing his solitude. Especially not someone who'd started flirting with him the moment she'd arrived.

Had she been flirting, though?

She'd quoted Jane Austen at him! She'd intimated that she'd taken one look at his castle and had fallen *in love* with him.

She was joking.

He wasn't laughing.

Except… He rubbed at an ache that stretched through his chest. While once upon a time she might've had stars in her eyes where he was concerned, there were no stars in her eyes now. *That* was a good thing.

He frowned, halting mid-rub. There were no

stars in Sadie's eyes, but nor was there pity or revulsion.

'So why don't we begin again?'

He started, realising he'd let the silence stretch too long.

'Hello, Enzo, it's nice to see you.'

She toasted him with her coffee, but he shook his head. 'Why don't we start with me apologising?'

Her hair was cut into a bob that bounced an inch above her shoulders, and she made a movement that sent it swishing, the dark strands catching the light. 'Absolutely! I'm good with that.'

The breezy bounce of her hair and good-natured satisfaction almost made him smile.

'Go on, then.' She set her coffee cup down and rubbed her hands together. 'Make it good.'

He did smile then; he even huffed out a laugh. He needed to work on that, because he didn't doubt that Sadie had been sent here by his family. And if he wanted her to give them a favourable report…

'Sadie, I apologise for my rudeness and for insinuating you were here for some nefarious purpose. I humbly beg your forgiveness.'

She seized her coffee cup again. 'Not bad. A six out of ten.'

He stiffened. 'What was wrong with it?' He'd always been a ten-out-of-ten guy.

'You didn't mean it.' Her distracting hair

swished some more. 'Oh, you meant the bit about the rudeness.'

'I meant it all!'

She surveyed him over the rim of her coffee, infuriatingly calm. 'You still think I'm here for nefarious purposes.'

He did his best not to focus on that infuriatingly distracting hair. 'I do not think you're here to seduce me.'

Despite her assurances, he knew how angry and ugly his scars looked. He also knew that some women didn't care what a man looked like—not when that man happened to bc as rich as Lorenzo Lombardi. But Sadie wasn't the kind of woman who'd pounce on a man when his defences were down. Sadie wasn't the kind of person who took advantage of anyone.

How do you know? You've had next to nothing to do with her for the last decade.

He knew because he knew Chelsea. He knew what a support Sadie had been to Chelsea when they'd been at boarding school together. A person didn't change that much. A person didn't go from being kind and caring to being only interested in all they could get. Chelsea wouldn't continue to talk about her with so much warmth, wouldn't continue to love her so much.

'But you do think I'm here to spy on you.'

Her eyes narrowed, and for no reason at all perspiration gathered on his top lip. 'Not spy. To check up on me.'

Tempting lips pursed.

Tempting? *What the hell...?* Maybe all of this solitude was sending him loopy. No amount of lecturing could stop him from watching in fascination as those very pretty lips un-pursed.

'Heaven forbid your family should be worried about you.'

Her words released him from the temporary spell. 'Are they worried?' He was no longer in hospital, no longer in a critical condition, no longer damaged beyond recognition. They should be relieved.

'I am, so they must be! I wasn't before landing on your door step, but to now find you so… malcontent.'

What did he have to be content about?

Financial security, the roof over your head, the fact you're alive?

He scowled.

'Naturally everyone was worried when the accident happened, and immediately afterwards. Everyone was beside themselves.'

Had she been beside herself?

'But, as soon as you were declared in a stable condition, my worry eased. I figured you'd have a tough and painful road ahead, but I also knew you to be strong and resilient.'

He felt neither of those things.

'So, when Chelsea started fretting and being a worrywart, I blamed pregnancy hormones.' A frown lodged in her eyes. 'Thankfully, though, she does actually want the toys she's sent me here to retrieve restored, and thankfully I've been itching to get inside your attics for as long as I've known about them, or she'd have come here herself.'

What the actual...? He swore.

'Exactly! Because this—' she pointed at him '—would not do a pregnant woman much good.'

'Dominic wouldn't have let her come.'

Sadie stared at him for two beats before seizing a huge strawberry and popping the entire thing in her mouth. He had a feeling she'd done it to stop from saying something…stinging, harsh, something she'd have to apologise for later.

She dabbed her mouth with a napkin when she was done. 'Chelsea and Dominic might be a loved-up duo, but he's not the boss of her.'

'That's not what I meant.'

'Are you sure? Because it's what you said.' Leaning forward, she peered at him with narrowed eyes. 'It's not a side of you I've ever considered.'

Something ugly shifted through him. 'Scales falling from your eyes?'

'Thick and fast,' she shot back cheerfully.

He was *not* his father or his grandfather. 'I am not some sexist jerk who thinks women should love, honour and *obey*, Sadie. I chose my words poorly. In saying Dominic wouldn't let Chelsea come, I merely meant he'd have tried to talk her out of it.'

Admittedly that might've been easier said than done, and he suspected the twist of his lips acknowledged as much. 'Barring that, he'd have come with her.' As a comfort and support, and to shield her from her stepbrother's bitterness.

'And you think that would've helped allay her worry?'

Not one iota. *Damn it.* He needed Sadie to send his family a good report. He didn't want them worrying about him, nor did he want them descending on him *en masse*. 'I'm sorry, Sadie. I'm cranky about everything, and have clearly been on my own too long. My manners have grown rusty.' He grimaced. 'It's been difficult to let off steam when I can't exercise. And one can't yell at the staff.'

'Especially when good staff are hard to come by, or so I'm told. I expect trying to replace staff who've walked out would be an utter bore.'

Her teasing nonsense had some of his tension easing. 'Beyond the pale,' he agreed. His father had yelled at the staff and Enzo refused to follow in those footsteps. 'You're the first person to breach the castle walls since my accident, I'm afraid, and that's made you a convenient target for all my built-up crankiness.' He hauled in a breath. 'I'm sorry. I'll try and do better from now on.'

'Okay, you just upgraded yourself to an eight out of ten.'

He tried to smile but it felt more like a wince.

'I'll keep my fingers crossed that the attics make my bad behaviour worth it.'

Her light laugh was balm to his bruised soul. 'I'm sure they will, and I'll upgrade your apology to an eight-point-five if you promise to show me them first thing tomorrow.'

'Done.' It seemed the least he could do.

She glanced at his leg, a question in her eyes. He bit back something surly. 'I've orders to exercise it. The stairs will do nicely. The doctors would approve.'

She let out a breath he hadn't realised she'd been holding. 'Okay, good.'

He stretched his bad leg out in front of him, tried not to wince at the aches and twinges and found a smile from somewhere. 'An eight-point-five isn't so bad.'

Her eyes danced. 'You're getting the hang of this "being an amiable host" gig. In another week, you'll be back to your usual charming self.'

He had to grit his teeth. Was she being deliberately irritating? Unclenching his jaw, he said, 'Speaking of being a considerate host, I'm sure you'd enjoy a chance to see your room and freshen up for dinner.' In roughly two hours' time… Surely that would give him enough time to shore up his defences and don a pleasant face?

On cue, Luisa appeared to show Sadie to her room. With a grin and a twinkle, Sadie followed her out. He found himself staring after her and shaking his head. He might need longer than two hours.

* * *

The grilling started at dinner. Expecting it, Enzo gritted his teeth and held his own in the tit-for-tat that ensued.

'When did the plaster come off your leg?'

'Three weeks ago. How are your grandparents?'

'Oh, muddling along, you know?' She gestured to his leg hidden beneath the table. 'You have exercises you have to do?'

'It's called rehab, Sadie. Exercises to increase strength and flexibility.'

She bit her lip. 'Does it hurt?'

He retorted with, 'Like the blazes some days,' and then wished he hadn't when her face fell.

'I *am* sorry, Enzo. It's so unfair.'

She had no idea how unfair, but he shrugged. 'It'll pass. The leg will get stronger.' He didn't want—or need—her face going soft like that.

As if sensing his discomfort, she became brisk again. 'Have you had any after-effects from the concussion?'

He gritted his teeth harder. 'No. And, Sadie, this is information my family already knows. You won't need it for your dossier.'

She gave a jaunty shrug. 'I like to dot my i's and cross my t's.' Spearing a piece of Luisa's excellent gnocchi on the end of her fork, she waved it through the air. 'Besides, this isn't for some fictional report. I'm asking because I'm curious and because I…care.'

She hesitated over that last word and he wondered why. He might've been a beast earlier, but they'd known each other a long time. If their positions had been reversed, he'd have cared about how she was doing too. If Chelsea asked him to check up on her…

Rolling his shoulders, he changed the topic. 'Where are you working now?'

'For a big auction house in Melbourne that specialises in antiques.'

'And you're working as a toy restorer?'

She gave a silent scream. 'I know! Crazy, isn't it?'

It was actually kind of perfect. Except… He fought a frown. 'I thought you wanted to open your own doll hospital?'

Her gaze promptly snapped away. 'So did I, but there's so much more variety at the auction house. Oh my God, you should see the treasures that come through.' She clasped a hand to her heart mock-dramatically. 'It's bliss.'

He fought a frown. She was lying. But *why*?

'Owning your own business is great in theory, but in practice…' She shook her head. 'Speaking of business, though… Yours?'

'Booming.'

Had she chickened out of setting up her own business?

'And is it true you've not seen your ex-girlfriend since the car crash?'

The question caught him off-guard. His hands clenched about his cutlery so hard, the ancient silver made divots in his palms. The ache in his fingers echoed the ache in his chest, and his leg. Somehow he kept his voice steady. 'Correct.' Thank God. He never wanted to clap eyes on Claudia again.

'The heartless piece of scum.' Sadie slammed her cutlery down. 'That narky collection of lark's vomit!'

He blinked at the inventive insults.

She tossed a few more into the mix—something about smelly toads and worms in compost heaps. Her shoulders deflated, though. 'I'm sorry she broke your heart, Enzo.'

Hold on. What? She'd broken his leg, not his heart.

'You deserved better.'

They were in agreement there. Before he could set her straight, though, she leaned across the table towards him and the gold flecks in her hazel eyes caught the light from the chandelier above and held him temporarily spellbound.

'Are you truly worried about how you look now?'

The words doused him in icy reality. He pulled on a mantle of forbidding hauteur. No one had dared ask him that question, and he hadn't thought Sadie would have the nerve to ask it either. A trickle of reluctant admiration filtered through him. He stamped it out. He thought it brave… Nonsense, it was rude! Except it didn't come across as rudeness. It came across as concern.

She raised her hands. 'I know, I know—skating

close to danger, on thin ice et cetera… It's just…' Her hands twisted together. 'One of the reasons I'm here, Enzo, is to, um…' She moistened her lips. 'To prepare you for the surprise birthday party Chelsea is planning to throw for you here in…um…four weeks' time.'

Chelsea was doing *what*? He shot to his feet.

Sadie pointed a finger at him. 'And you can't let on that you know.'

Enzo didn't say a word. He turned on his heel and stormed out.

CHAPTER TWO

SADIE SWEPT INTO Enzo's gloomy living room at eight a.m. the next morning and let out the breath she'd been holding. He hadn't put in an appearance at breakfast and she'd wondered if he'd spend the entire day avoiding her. But here he was, looking admittedly stormy and scowling, but most definitely present in the flesh.

A sigh welled through her. That flesh might be a bit battered and bruised, but what she'd said yesterday still held true. Those scars—even as fresh and angry as they were—not only *didn't* detract from Enzo's magnetic masculinity, they enhanced it.

His face had always been impossibly beautiful. It could've been used in scientific textbooks to illustrate beauty's principle of symmetry. In marring that ideal of perfect symmetry, his scars gave him an uncompromising ruggedness that only enhanced his other…advantages.

She gazed now at the imposing height, the broad shoulders, deep chest and muscled torso, and another sigh welled through her. Enzo still had the power to make a grown woman weak at the knees. She braced her legs and refused to allow them a single tiny wobble. *Ahem.* She wouldn't allow them *two* wobbles; one was understandable.

Instead of focusing on his advantages, she focused on his scowl. 'Let me guess—you're not a morning person?'

His jaw tightened. 'And a good morning to you too, Sadie.'

'Oh!' She feigned shock. 'After the way you stormed away last night, I didn't think we were bothering with manners any more.'

Dark eyes narrowed, but she merely beamed. 'But it's a new day, the sun is shining, manners are once again flavour of the month and it feels as if anything is possible!'

Closing his eyes, he rubbed a fist across his brow. She suspected he was counting to ten.

'Headache coming on?'

His eyes snapped open. *Uh-huh.* She probably deserved that glare, but she refused to tremble beneath its force. Enzo might be cranky and out of sorts and, if what Sadie thought was true, nursing a broken heart from the dastardly Claudia; he'd gone deathly pale when she'd mentioned Claudia's name last night. But buried beneath all of that was the kind heart she remembered from her teenage years.

More importantly, buried beneath all that grumpiness was the brother Chelsea adored. And, as

Chelsea was the sister Sadie had never had, she'd do whatever she could to uncover him again. But a more softly-softly approach might be called for.

'Perhaps you should take some paracetamol.'

'Already loaded to the hilt.'

She crossed her fingers and held them up for him to see. 'Hopefully it'll kick in soon and give you some relief.' When he didn't say anything, she tried to contain an excited wriggle. 'So the fact you're actually here… Does that mean we can head straight up to the attics?'

He shook his head, not in refusal, but a kind of bemusement.

'If I say pretty, *pretty* please with a cherry on top?'

'As it appears I'll get no peace until I do…' He hitched his head in the direction of the stairs. 'Follow me.'

She kept her tone deliberately light. 'Are you really expecting peace while I'm here, Enzo?'

They were halfway up the first set of stairs and he swung round so fast she feared his bad leg wouldn't hold him. She shot her arms out ready to catch him.

The mouth that had opened—no doubt to utter something cutting—closed again. '*What* are you doing?'

'Getting ready to catch you. I didn't know if your leg would cope with you spinning around like that.'

His jaw went slack. 'Sadie, if I am in danger of falling, get out of the way. I'd squash you flat!'

'I'm stronger than I look.' And he wasn't going to do any additional damage to himself; not while she was here. She'd never be able to look Chelsea in the eye again. 'I reckon I could prop you up long enough for you to get your balance again.'

He muttered something under his breath in Italian.

'But you didn't lose your balance; you didn't fall over.' She patted him on the shoulder. 'Good for you.' Which sounded patronising, when she didn't mean it to, but she was so darned relieved he hadn't hurt himself…

Oh! The heat from his shoulder collided with her palm in a scorching, dizzying wave, and she reefed her hand away. Enzo's shoulder was rock hard and agonisingly tempting beneath his shirt.

What the hell? No way! She wasn't going to tread that same old, tired road again. She could admire his masculine beauty, but that was where it stopped.

'The girl I used to know was kind of quiet and shy.' She glanced up to find Enzo glaring at her.

'While the guy I used to know would never have glared at me like that.' She waggled her eyebrows. 'Looks like none of our expectations are coming true. More surprises are probably hovering on the horizon just out of sight. Energising, isn't it?'

Nothing—not even the smallest of smiles. She

planted her hands on her hips. 'So you not only broke your leg in that car accident, but your sense of humour too, huh?'

His eyes narrowed.

'Never mind, I expect with some concerted rehabilitation it can be resurrected.'

'You're relentless, aren't you?'

'Like water torture.' With a wink, she slipped past him to skip up the rest of the stairs. 'Come on, slow coach, the attics await!'

He followed, grumbling, but she swore she glimpsed a brief smile.

'Turn left at the top,' he instructed.

'What's on this level?'

'Bedrooms, mostly.'

They climbed another set of stairs. 'My bedroom is on this level.'

She glanced over her shoulder. Had he deliberately placed her on the floor that was furthest from him and the rest of the house—or, rather, castle?

Glancing up, he hesitated. 'Your room isn't as large as the rooms on the second floor, but it has one of the best views of the sea, and I thought you'd like it.'

Things inside her turned gooey. *No melting...* 'The view is out of this world. And, Enzo, my bedroom is enormous and perfection in every way.' He'd taken the trouble of giving her a room he thought she'd like. The old Enzo was still there, even if he was trapped under something heavy.

They continued climbing to the next floor. 'The old servants' quarters are on this level, and then…' Enzo led her to a half-staircase with a landing and two doors at the top. 'The attics.' He gestured at the doors—one to the left and the other to the right. 'Which one do you want to go through first?'

'This one on the…right!'

Enzo pushed open the right-hand door and ushered her inside. She stood just inside the doorway to clasp her hands beneath her chin, her gaze wandering over the assorted boxes and items of furniture that greeted her. Three big dormer windows flooded the room with light, ensuring it was neither dank nor dark.

'I thought you'd be rifling through boxes and pulling off dust covers by now.'

'This is a moment to be savoured. In this moment, anything feels possible. I don't yet know what delicious treasures might be found.'

'There won't be anything of value. My father picked the attics clean years ago.'

'Pfft, what did your father know? He was an idiot. And look!' With a laugh, she pounced on an old-fashioned paddle ball, the rubber string still intact. Swinging round, she sent the rubber ball arcing towards him, pulling it back at the last moment so as to not hit him.

To his credit, Enzo didn't even flinch. Dropping it back into the box, she emerged with a Rubik's Cube. Without warning, she tossed it to him and he caught it without dropping his walking stick.

'What the hell, Sadie?'

She slid him a grin. 'The accident didn't affect your reflexes. *That* needs to go in my report.'

This time he finally smiled properly, as if he couldn't help it, and it sent a bigger surge of adrenaline through her than the attic had done. Enzo's problem was he'd been left to his own devices for too long. He needed a bit of convivial company to jolly him up and get him out of his own head for a bit. Admittedly, he had a lot of reasons for feeling down in the dumps, but brooding didn't do anybody any good.

'Well, I'll leave you to explore and—'

'Oh no, you don't.' She'd noted the way he'd started to lean more heavily on that cane of his. 'Please sit here and keep me company.'

Pulling a dust cover off what looked like an old dining-room chair—its embroidered seat now a little worse for wear—she tested its strength then patted its seat.

'I don't need a rest, Sadie.'

'Which is just as well because, eventually, we're both going to have to trudge down all of those stairs again. But I have no ulterior motive, other than the fact that I might need your manly muscles to help me move some boxes.'

To her surprise, he did as she bid. 'I'll stay if you answer a question for me.'

'Deal!'

'What really happened with your doll hospital idea?'

She tried not to fidget under that piercing gaze. 'Like I said last night, nothing, really. It just seemed a bit risky.'

She recalled the looks of horror on her grandparents' faces when she'd outlined her plan to them, and swallowed. They'd lost no time pointing out all the reasons it would be too risky, too challenging, too *ambitious.* She stuffed down the sigh that rose through her. 'I put it on the back burner, and decided to get some experience in the workforce first.'

'It wouldn't have been a huge outlay to start up a business like that.'

It still would've taken all she'd had.

'If you need a backer, I'd be happy to invest in your business.'

She swung back, probably with her mouth unflatteringly ajar, wondering if she'd heard him correctly.

'You have what it takes to make a business successful, Sadie.'

Did she?

'A specialised, in-demand skill…and passion.'

That word filtered through her: *passion.* How long had it been since she'd truly embraced her passions rather than try to diminish or ignore them? And how long had it been since someone had truly believed in her, shown faith in her, the way Enzo just had? And he hadn't seen her in years.

'Sadie?'

She shook herself. 'Bless your boots, Enzo. That's such a generous offer.'

'But you're not going to accept it?'

She shook her head.

'Because of your pride?'

Because her life was in flux; because she'd packed up all her things in Australia with no plans to return any time soon. But she didn't want to talk about that. She didn't even want to think about it. 'Because, while I'd be prepared to risk my own money, I'm not risking anyone else's.'

'I have a lot of money. I can afford to lose some.'

She stared down her nose at him. 'Are you boasting?'

'Just stating facts.'

That made her laugh. Simple fact of the matter was, she'd lost her nerve for starting up her own business. If she'd been truly passionate about her doll hospital, she wouldn't have let anyone talk her out of it.

Something inside her threatened to lift its head and come back to life, but she patted it kindly and told it to go back to sleep.

'If you change your mind…'

'Thanks, Enzo, that's kind of you.'

She wouldn't change her mind, though, and she hoped he'd let the matter drop. Her shoulders might've actually sagged when he said, 'So, how are you going to do this? Is there a method to your treasure hunting or are you all magpie randomness?'

'I have a treasure map!' She pulled out her phone with a flourish. 'Courtesy of Chelsea. I need to find the piano with a bust of someone important-looking balanced on top.'

'Galileo, perhaps?'

She followed his finger to where it pointed. 'Aha! I need to keep it on my left and take eight steps towards a 1950s pram before then turning right at the trunk made of alligator hide.' She followed Chelsea's instructions. 'Now, somewhere here there ought to be a box full of linen, and behind that…eureka! Here's the tan suitcase.'

She held it aloft like a trophy and then trudged back to where he sat. Grabbing a little wooden stool, she plonked herself across from him and set the suitcase between them. 'Buried treasure duly found.'

'Chelsea hid it for you to find?' He gaped at her. *'Why?'*

'Because…fun.' She spread her hands. Didn't he ever do anything just for fun?

At the word fun, he scowled again. 'Look, Sadie, about this party…'

She leapt up to poke about some bits and bobs nearby—including a vanity case and a men's jewellery box. 'The one that Chelsea is throwing for you?'

'What other party would I be referring to?'

Mischief shuffled through her. 'Oh, your mother hasn't mentioned the ball she's giving to raise funds for homeless women? She's counting on your attendance. It's not until November, though. And your stepfather has organised a box at…let me think…is it AC Milan or Inter Milan? Anyway, there's some huge football day out. Then of course there'll be the baby shower once Chelsea's littlie arrives.'

'Very funny. I actually believed you for a moment.'

She set the vanity case and jewellery box beside the suitcase and sat on the stool again. 'What gave me away?'

'Stephen hates football. Cricket is what he loves—a game I truly don't understand. But back to this party Chelsea has her heart set on—it *cannot* happen. You need to find a way to stop it.'

'I see no need for that. Why would I want to spoil her fun? Why would you?'

His jaw clenched. 'It's *my* birthday!'

She gestured to the suitcase. 'You own whatever's inside that suitcase, but you don't seem to begrudge its contents to Chelsea. She said you'd told her to take whatever she fancied from up here.'

He glanced at the suitcase and his frown deepened. 'I told her to take anything she wanted. Why did she leave it behind?'

'Her email answers that. Here, listen to this…' She scrolled down to Chelsea's initial message. '"Enzo told me to help myself to anything I wanted, and as soon as I saw these I wanted them with my every atom. But I didn't want to jinx this pregnancy, not after finding out what had happened to Mum. So I gathered them up, put them in the tan suitcase and hid them, not wanting to count my chickens".'

'When did she do this?'

'The first time she visited the castle. So, when was that…two years ago?' That was when Enzo's horrid father had died, leaving him this not-so-humble pile of rocks.

His stare remained steady. 'What did Chelsea find out about her mother?'

Sadie wasn't sure it was her place to say. Chelsea hadn't sworn her to secrecy or anything. Actually, she was surprised Enzo didn't know already.

'Sadie?'

'She found out her mother had had several miscarriages. One before she was born and two after. She found these—' she pointed at the suitcase indicating its contents '—before she and Dominic married.'

'And before becoming pregnant.'

'Exactly. But unlike her mother she hasn't had an early-stage miscarriage. She's nearly five months gone and in the best of health,' she added, because there were new shadows in his eyes and she wanted to eliminate them as soon as she could. 'She's in the hands of an excellent doctor who's aware of her mother's history. She's being monitored carefully and coddled appropriately. There's no reason why her pregnancy won't go full-term.'

He blew out of breath. 'Good. Right.'

That was the moment Sadie saw what he held in his hand—that Rubik's Cube she'd tossed to him earlier, except now it was solved. Reaching out, she took it and turned it over and over in her hands—each side was a perfect square of colour. 'How did you do that? I could never figure these out.'

'It's just a puzzle.'

She handed it back to him. 'If you're clever enough to solve a Rubik's Cube, Enzo, then I expect you also have the smarts to convince everyone you're having fun at a party you don't really want.'

Except the energy it would require of him and the unwanted intrusion into his solitude left Enzo feeling unutterably heavy. He didn't *want* to celebrate anything—least of all another journey around the sun.

'There's a bit more in Chelsea's message you should probably hear.'

He glanced back at Sadie. She had a smudge of dirt on one cheek, but both her cheeks glowed with good health, and her eyes shone. Was it because she loved attics? It seemed such an innocent thing to love. Maybe he'd spent too much time in the company of women who had left him feeling jaded—women like Claudia—but it was hard to trust in anything as innocent as someone's enjoyment in exploring the contents of attics that didn't belong to them.

There was no denying Sadie's enjoyment, though. Her eyes sparkled, and every now and again she'd shimmy as if she couldn't help it. But was that enjoyment innocent? Did she somehow mean to profit from his attics? And, if she did, did he care?

He cared nothing for these things per se. If he'd needed the space, he'd just as soon have carried everything down to the incinerator and burned it. So if anyone he knew wanted the contents of his attics, shouldn't he be happy just to let them take it?

Recent events, though, had burned the generosity from his soul. He now found himself hungering to punish anyone who wanted to take advantage of him. Another part of him hated himself for this attitude, for his suspicions.

Sadie isn't trying to take advantage of you.

She was at the castle with an ulterior motive.

Sì*, to help you.*

He didn't want help. He didn't want company. He didn't want a party! He wanted to be left alone to recover his strength, to process all that had happened and to solder the broken bits of himself back together. What he didn't want was sparkling eyes, glossy hair and lips so pretty they made him wonder what it would be like to kiss them.

Again...

His chest clenched. He'd never forgotten the kiss he and Sadie had shared all those years ago.

Not relevant!

He shook himself impatiently. After recent events, he'd sworn never again to embark on a serious relationship. He wasn't going to give any woman the power or opportunity to pull a Claudia-sized tantrum on him. He wasn't going to give any woman the chance to ruin his life.

How do you feel about unserious relationships, fleeting flings, temporary hook-ups?

He blinked. His mouth went dry. In the next moment, reality hit. He was not going to *hook up fleetingly* with his stepsister's best friend. *That* had the potential to lead to trouble. His mother had suffered enough domestic disharmony at his father's hands to last a lifetime. He'd sworn never to do anything to disrupt her current happiness. She deserved to enjoy her hard-won peace.

'Enzo.'

He started at the sharp note in Sadie's voice.

'You were miles away.'

And, from her look, wherever his mind had been, she hadn't considered it either pleasant or happy.

Welcome to my life.

'I apologise for my inattention.' If memory served, she'd wanted to tell him something—no doubt something he didn't want to hear.

Instead, she leapt to her feet. 'Come on; today

is for fun. Let's take our treasure downstairs and admire it properly.'

It was the last thing he'd expected. 'But you've hardly looked at anything.'

'Not true.' She gestured to the bounty at their feet. 'I'll get to work properly tomorrow. Like I said, today is just for fun.'

'Isn't there anything else you want to take downstairs?' He could carry more than the suitcase.

'Well, as tempting as I find that beautiful treadle sewing machine over there, it's far too heavy for us to carry downstairs.' Her smile widened and she bent down to pat the suitcase. 'Besides, I expect to find plenty in here to keep me occupied.'

She handed it to him, before gathering up the vanity case and jewellery box. Had Chelsea given her treasure-map directions to them as well?

At the last moment, she settled them on top of a box that she hefted into her arms. 'How's a girl supposed to resist a miscellaneous box of odds and ends, I ask you?'

Suppressing a smile, he ushered her out of the door. It wasn't until they were standing on the landing and facing the door opposite that he realised what her earlier revelation also indicated. 'If you knew that Chelsea's so-called treasure was through the right-hand door, that means you also knew the toy collection is through the left one.'

'Rumbled!'

He pointed. '*That* has to be the attic you're actually dying to get inside.'

'It is.'

'Then why…?'

Her hands were full of box, but one finger uncurled to point at the suitcase. 'Enzo, there are toys inside that. Chelsea wants me to restore them for her children—as long as I have your permission to do so.'

Of course she had his permission.

'*That's* why I'm really here. What's behind the left-hand door will satisfy professional curiosity. It can wait.'

Not just professional curiosity but her own personal curiosity too, he imagined. Sadie had been obsessed with antique toys ever since he'd known her. It occurred to him now, though, that he didn't know why. And why the hell hadn't she pursued her dream to open her own doll hospital?

He glanced at the closed attic door and then at the suitcase he held, and his lips twisted as he twigged what she was up to. 'You're putting Chelsea's needs before your own.'

She frowned at whatever she saw in his face. 'I'm not sure what you're getting at. I'm going to enjoy—'

'It's a little heavy-handed, don't you think—all of this leading by example? It must be wearing.'

She blinked.

'I am *not* having a party, Sadie. I won't have my house invaded and me paraded like a circus exhibit. If Chelsea persists with the idea, then I'll vacate the premises and she and whoever she invites can party without me.'

He turned and started down the stairs, swearing he heard her mutter, 'Selfish pig,' under her breath. He didn't give a flying fig what she thought of him. Nevertheless, the insult burrowed under his skin to prickle and burn.

He swung back, his hand gripping his cane so tightly, his fingers started to ache. 'What she should be doing is looking after herself and preparing for the arrival of her baby!' Not jumping on a plane from London and hiking it across to his isolated castle.

'Has it not occurred to you that might be exactly what she's doing in throwing this party?'

'Don't be daft! She's doing it out of some misplaced sense of responsibility!'

'I see.'

Ice dripped from her voice. In the past, he'd considered her quiet and shy, but never icy. Beneath her reserve she'd always been as warm and comforting as *risotto alle Milanese*—his favourite dish. For reasons he couldn't fathom, this new iciness infuriated him.

'Why are you really here, Sadie? What are you hoping to gain by rifling through my attics?' He barely recognised the mocking fury in his voice, but he couldn't stop the hot rush of words. 'Are you hoping to win kudos and a healthy commission from your auction house for an as-yet-undiscovered treasure?'

She didn't utter a single word of protest, but her mouth had gone thin and she eyed him, the suitcase and his stick with a wariness that cut him to the quick.

'Do you mind if I get past?'

He immediately pressed himself against the wall to let her slip by, his heart slugging against his ribs while nausea churned in his gut. He forced himself down the steps after her, keeping a reasonable and respectable distance. The accusations he'd flung at her had been vile. And the *way* he'd flung them at her…

She was halfway along the corridor when he finally made it to the bottom. 'Sadie.'

She halted and turned, but she didn't move back towards him.

'I know I sounded fierce just then. But…' His heart thundered. 'You have to know I'd never hurt you.'

Her eyes flashed. 'No. I *don't* know that. I don't know you at all any more, Enzo.' Her face fell. 'What happened to you?'

He remained silent, but a chasm opened in his chest. Had he truly frightened her? If he had, it'd be unforgivable. What the hell kind of person was he in danger of becoming?

'I know you're in pain.' She pointed to his leg before touching a hand to her chest above her heart. 'But that's no excuse for directing your anger at me. Certainly not with the kind of force you just did. Your accusations are not only unfounded, but unforgivable.'

Her words stabbed him like knives, each of them finding their mark.

'Chelsea is one of the most important people in my life. Your family have never been anything other than welcoming and kind to me. To think I would ever seek to profit from that financially…' She lifted her chin. '*No!* That's more a reflection on you than me.'

True; all of it was true. A hard, cold lump the size of a gravestone lodged in his chest. He was in danger of turning into his father. Not in a million years would he have thought himself capable of that.

'But you haven't just insulted me, you insult Chelsea too. "Some misplaced sense of responsibility"—that's what you called it. She loves you, Lorenzo, with all of her heart. She considers you her brother. *Some misplaced sense of responsibility.* Is that how you feel about her?'

'No,' he croaked. He adored Chelsea. He'd walk over hot coals for her.

He set the suitcase down and braced a hand against the wall, concentrating on his breathing, concentrating on stopping the corridor from swaying. Selfish and self-absorbed, was what he'd become.

'Do you need help down the stairs?'

He shook his head. He didn't deserve her help.

The corridor stopped swaying and he forced himself upright. 'Sadie…'

'Me coming here was a terrible mistake, but it's one I can rectify.'

She turned on her heel and disappeared down the stairs.

Enzo limped back to the attic stairs, lowered himself down to them and dropped his head to his hands.

CHAPTER THREE

STOMP! STOMP! STOMP!

Sadie followed the clifftop path down to the beach at its base. Slamming hands onto her hips, she glared at the crescent of golden sand, at the soft sapphire sea and the inviting shade beneath the pine trees that fringed this exquisite beach—all of it utterly glorious.

Sadly, she wasn't going to get to enjoy any of it. Spinning on her heel, she stomped back up the path—*thump, thump, thump.* By the time she'd reached the top, some of the oomph had gone out of her fury.

Okay, enough with steps for one day. Would anyone notice if she melted onto the soft grass and stared at the sky for a while to catch her breath and give her legs a chance to recover their strength? It was only the thought that Enzo might be watching from one of his castle's many windows that prevented her from doing any such thing. Gritting her teeth, she forced her legs across the lawn in the direction of the terrace.

The terrace was a paved expanse that ran the

full length of the castle. Curving gently, it formed a generous semi-circle at the castle's rear. Planters of various sizes were dotted about, filled with colourful flowers, screening hedge plants and several strategically placed pencil pines, all of which helped to demarcate and complement the different seating areas on offer—large and small, open and private—all sharing that enviable view.

It was only when Enzo stood from one of the tables that she realised he'd been watching from much closer quarters than a window above. On the table in front of him sat a jug of water, moisture condensing its sides. Her mouth fell to its knees and begged for mercy. Who knew stomping could be such thirsty work? But, rather than race over to pour the contents of the pitcher down her throat—or over her head to cool her overheated flesh—she halted and folded her arms.

'Sadie, will you please do me the kindness of joining me?'

She had a flight to book and bags to pack.

'Please give me an opportunity to apologise to you properly…' He hesitated. 'And comprehensively.'

That final word emerged reluctantly, as if he'd had to force it out. *Good.*

He poured a generous glass of water, ice tinkling temptingly, and set it in front of the other chair. 'It's a hot day, and you must be thirsty after your walk.'

With a huff, she stalked over to the table, reached

for that alluring glass and took a long, satisfying drink before sitting. *For Chelsea.* 'Just so you know, I'm doing this for the water, not for you.'

'Noted,' he said, though she suspected her childish gibe had him fighting a smile.

If he laughed at her, she'd get up, walk away and leave—end of story. She'd always known she wasn't good enough for the likes of Enzo Lombardi and his peers. At unbidden moments his mother's words still sounded through her and they still had the power to make her flinch.

Sadie is not from our world. This has to stop. She doesn't have the resources to negotiate the world you come from.

These days, though, she didn't have to put up with such snooty attitudes.

Enzo's not like that.

Of course he was. Chelsea wasn't like that, though. Chelsea was an utter sweetheart. At the thought of her friend, her heart sank. Was she really going to let her down? She hitched it back up. She wasn't—*Enzo* was.

She took another sip of water while Enzo remained chafingly silent. She lifted her glass in his direction. 'Just so you know, I'll be leaving as soon as I finish this.'

Which meant he had the time it would take her to drink half a glass of water to properly and comprehensively apologise. She crossed her fingers beneath the table and hoped that he could manage it.

When Enzo had yelled at her just then on the attic stairs, his face contorting with fury, it had been like a knife to the heart from the boy she'd once adored. She knew her girlhood crush on Enzo had been nothing more than immature longings and fantasies—insubstantial and not based in any kind of reality. But one of the things she cherished from those long-ago memories was the fact that Enzo had always been kind to her. He'd always treated her with respect.

Until that stupid kiss at that stupid ball when she'd been eighteen. A kiss that had burned itself on her brain. A kiss she'd never been able to forget. His subsequent withdrawal had been the exception to the rule—and even then he hadn't been unkind, just…aloof. But this morning it had occurred to her that maybe it was all his former kindness that had been the exception, and some silly, long-ago part of her heart had broken.

She'd wanted to leave and never see him again, and now she could. Draining her glass, she set it on the table with a decisive click and rose. 'I'd like to say it's been a pleasure, but we both know that'd be a lie. Goodbye, Enzo—'

'Oh God, don't leave. I'm sorry. I'm struggling to find words to explain myself. I can't find any that will…that are halfway polite. Damn it, Sadie, I don't recognise myself when I look in the mirror any more. I *hate* what I see!'

His chest rose and fell as if he'd been running,

and his eyes flashed, but he held her gaze. A lump lodged in her throat.

'I didn't know vanity was one of my besetting sins and…'

And...?

'I'm angry with myself for being so shallow.'

She turned his words over. She'd never considered him vain, though clearly that was the interpretation he'd arrived at, and had found himself wanting as a result.

'The thought of having a party where people are going to look at me as less than I was, as an object to be pitied, feeling sorry for me… I can't stand it.'

'That's not vanity, Enzo,' she said slowly, shaking her head. 'That's pride.' And that was something she could understand.

He scratched a hand over his jaw, a jaw currently darkened by an intriguing stubble. 'Will you let me pour you another glass of water? Or half a glass?' he added when she didn't immediately answer.

Her thirst was nowhere near quenched, but she refused to capitulate quickly or easily. 'Half a glass.' She took her seat.

He dragged in a breath. 'I knew you were coming to the *castello*, and I thought I was prepared, but I didn't realise someone intruding on my solitude would have such an impact on me.'

'Impact how?'

'I thought you'd be as quiet and reserved and shy as you always were. But you're not.'

He'd thought she'd be easy company—as in, easy to ignore. Had he expected her to be soothing and sympathetic? He'd have loathed her sympathy and viewed all attempts at being soothed with suspicion. She sipped her water. 'You thought I'd tiptoe gently around you like everyone else has done.'

'I suppose I did.'

'You've had plenty of people coming in to mop your fevered brow. You're on the road to recovery now and no longer a patient. I didn't think you'd appreciate it if I came in all softly-softly and treated you like you weren't capable of looking after yourself.'

'*That* would've been appalling.'

She spread her hands, silently asking what was the problem, then?

He scowled. 'Instead you came in all demanding, turning everything on its head, and *impossible* to ignore.'

'*That's* why you lost your temper and shouted like you did?'

He rubbed a hand over his face, grinding back an impatient sound. 'I did *that* because you wouldn't listen to me. I said no to the party—told you I didn't want one—but you blatantly ignored me.'

Her heart started beating too hard.

'My fear since the accident is losing my autonomy.' His lips twisted. 'When I was lying in a hospital bed, my leg in traction and my mind groggy from the concussion, in my more lucid moments I wondered if I'd ever be independent again. The thought that I might not be had me wanting to die.'

Her hand flew to her mouth.

'And, when you didn't listen to me, it felt as if I was losing control—in danger of once again forfeiting my autonomy.'

His words not only took the wind out of her proverbial sails, they left her becalmed. She'd made him feel worse when he was already struggling with his self-image, and she hated herself for it. 'I'm sorry, Enzo. Truly sorry. I didn't mean to make you feel that way.'

He stared back. His jaw clenched. 'How do you do that?'

Do what?

'Give a ten-out-of-ten apology just like that.' He snapped his fingers. 'And I'm not looking for an apology. I know you didn't mean to make me feel like that. If I'd been in a better frame of mind, I'd have bitten my tongue and counted to ten. Instead I yelled at you like a damn brute. And the look on your face…' He forked a hand through his hair. 'I'll never forget it. I'm sorry I frightened you. I promise to never yell at you again or—'

He broke off, breathing hard. 'Sadie, I hope to God you know I'd never lay a finger on you; that I'd never hurt you.'

'Of course I know that!' And she did. It'd been her own foolish heart and memories she'd fled from, not him.

His eyes narrowed, as if he didn't quite believe her. 'I acted like a bully.'

She'd had to deal with bullies most of her life. The girls at boarding school had made her life an absolute misery. If it hadn't been for Chelsea, she didn't know what she'd have done. That quiet, vicious bullying that had let her know she'd never belong, never be one of them, never be enough, had been relentless and awful. To be so constantly undermined…

Enzo might not think her good enough, might not think she belonged in his world, but he'd never say such a thing out loud. His temper had shocked her, but she hadn't felt bullied, and nor had she felt afraid for her well-being. 'You know what I think? I think your life these last few months has been too fraught, too heavy and dark. You need to learn to cultivate a sense of insouciance again.'

One corner of his mouth hooked up. *'Insouciance?'*

'What? It's a beautiful word. And so much more exotic than "equanimity" or plain old "balance".'

'Is that what you are these days—insouciant?'

'And bright and breezy.'

'Whatever it is…' his lips relaxed into a smile '…it looks good on you, Sadie.'

His gaze was full of warmth and appreciation

and she found herself wanting to bask under it. Their gazes caught and held for a fraction too long. With a jolt, she dragged hers away. 'Flatterer.'

'Flattery is better than intimidation.'

'See, you're getting the hang of it already. Keep this up and we'll have you bright and breezy and insouciant in no time at all.'

But would they? She recalled the expression on his face when she'd mentioned Claudia's name last night—how haunted and lost he'd looked, how pale and tense he'd gone. It had made her stomach churn. 'Do you want to know how I got over my crush on you, Enzo?' she blurted out, apropos of nothing.

He blinked, but then his gaze sharpened. 'I'd very much like to know.'

Hers had been a schoolgirl crush, while whatever he'd felt for Claudia had been far more mature, but maybe she could say something to help him find a path out of his heartbreak. 'My life was on the point of change that last summer I spent with your family.'

'You were heading off to university.'

She'd spent several weeks each summer with Chelsea's family whilst at boarding school. They were warm, idyllic days just hanging out with Chelsea—and often Enzo as well—swimming, sunbathing and playing tennis. By the time she went to university, she hadn't had to deal with the mean girls from boarding school *and* she'd been able to indulge her love of history and art while discovering other things she'd also come to love. 'I threw myself into the experience.'

'What do you mean?'

'I mean, I wasn't there to simply tick off a list to achieve a qualification. I *loved* what I was studying—I had a new passion to focus on.'

'I can see how that would be helpful.'

Did he, though? 'I joined clubs.' Fun people had actively enlisted her. It had been so inclusive. 'The hockey club, the history club, a book group… And I worked two part-time jobs so I could afford to move out into a shared house.' She'd made herself too busy to brood endlessly about Enzo.

'Independence is a great experience.'

'It meant I could stay out as late as I wanted.'

He huffed out a laugh. 'Meaning you dated.'

'Of course I did.' More importantly, she'd become her own person.

'And it helped?'

She slid him a mischievous grin. 'Depends on which dates we're talking about.' She was quiet for a moment. 'Before university, I always saw my life as a bit grey. Spending the summers with your family was the one bright spot in my life.'

He frowned. 'I never knew that.'

'Why should you? What I'm trying to say, Enzo, is that, when I had the opportunity to, I surrounded myself with all the things I loved that brought me energy and enthusiasm and filled my life with colour.'

He stared at her for a long moment. 'So…you're not-so-subtly telling me that I should surround myself with colour?'

Surely it was better than grey?

His face went tight. 'Your teenage crush is a different beast from what I've had to endure in recent months.'

'I know, but…'

'It's naïve to think that I can simply snap my fingers and— '

He broke off, breathing hard, and it was all she could do not to cry. Because, whatever else this Claudia had been, she hadn't deserved this man's love.

'But I do not wish to argue with you again. Let's agree to disagree.'

So much for trying to help. 'Fine, but here's something else for you to chew over: you *do* have your independence; you *haven't* lost your autonomy. You have the kind of money to take your life in whatever direction you want. That has to feel liberating.'

He stared at her. 'I…'

Enough already. 'I accept your apology, Enzo. Thank you for explaining all of that to me.'

He eyed her warily. 'And you'll stay?'

She hesitated. 'The party…?'

His gaze snapped away from hers and he stared

out at the horizon, his mouth a grim line. He really didn't want a party, did he?

'And by "party" I mean a small and intimate affair with only family and close friends—not thrill-seekers coming to gawk.'

He grimaced.

'Enzo, do you really think it unreasonable that your family want to celebrate the fact that you're still here to celebrate with?'

'What if I promise to think about it?'

'That would be both generous and good-natured of you.' Reaching across, she filled her glass to the very brim. 'Thank you. I'd love to stay.'

Enzo closed his eyes and let out a breath. Sadie was going to stay. From now on he needed to be more careful, more measured. A party might be anathema to him, but so was worrying Chelsea, especially when she was pregnant.

He had no doubt that Sadie would've made light of the incident, would've assured Chelsea all was well and probably just said something along the lines that he was fine and simply needed more time to adjust or something. But Chelsea would've read between the lines. If Sadie had left, it would've sent Chelsea into a tizz. She'd have insisted on coming to see him. On top of everything else, he'd have had an over-protective, eagle-eyed little sister to deal with as well. One who read far too much into everything he did and everything he said.

His temples started to throb. It'd be preferable for Sadie to stay for her allotted two weeks. She could send favourable reports back to Chelsea on his progress and welfare, while he came up with a way to gently extricate himself from the party. He'd be careful to make sure Chelsea never knew that Sadie had told him about it either. He wouldn't betray Sadie and cause trouble between the two women. They meant a lot to each other and he had no intention of messing with that. But he had no intention of having a party either.

For the next two weeks Sadie could poke away in the attics to her heart's content. He'd find things to keep him busy during the day and all that would be required of him would be a few hours with Sadie in the evening—a bit of conversation… Maybe Sadie would like to watch TV or read a book, and then he could pretend to watch or read too. Not ideal, but not the end of the world. And temporary—*very* temporary. He could muster the resources to grin and bear it.

He glanced at Sadie from the corner of his eyes. Time to don his 'good host' manners and show her some additional reasons why staying here—temporarily—could be just the ticket. Sadie going home relaxed and rested would convince Chelsea more than words ever could that all was well at the castle.

He knew she'd seen the beach… 'Have you stumbled upon the pool house yet?'

Her gaze swung from where she contemplated

the view, and the summer sun picked out the amber flecks in her eyes. She'd once described her eyes as a muddy green, but there was nothing muddy about them. The cool green and that startling amber had him thinking of shady forest groves or of diving into a still sea to swim in a forest of kelp.

'You have a pool?'

'Not just a pool, a pool *house*—an entire entertainment complex.' He did his best to stop his lips from twisting.

'Who needs a pool when…?' She waved a hand towards the sea.

'Come and see.' Maybe then she'd realise.

Draining the contents of her glass, she stood and gestured for him to lead the way. He took her to a building on the other side of the garden, and the expression on her face when he led her inside had him biting back a smile. The sun flooding through the arched windows at this time of day, and bouncing off marble, crystal, cut-glass and gold-gilt furniture, could be a bit much.

The light danced on the water of the thirty-foot pool, as it did on the tiled fresco of mermaids that decorated its base, while the individual pendants of the three chandeliers that hung above it twinkled with a narcissistic brilliance. The furniture arranged around the pool's perimeter—all glass, white leather and gold gilt—likewise gleamed with an indulgent lustre. The entire enterprise boasted extravagance, excess and wealth.

He loathed it.

The view through the wall of glass, however, was unparalleled.

They watched a sleek white yacht glide by on the turquoise water below and only when it had passed did Sadie turn to him. 'This looks like something from a movie set.'

'It's been used in two Italian films and a French one.'

'I suppose the benefit of this is one can swim all year round if one wants. Because, of course, it's heated?'

That last was phrased more as a question than a statement, and he nodded.

Her eyes lit with sudden mischief. 'And one could have some rather fine parties here.'

He was *not* having a pool party.

'What's through there?' She pointed to two doors in the far wall.

Striding across, he opened the first one. 'Ladies and gents shower rooms.'

She shrugged, as if to say, *of course*.

He led her through the other door to a games room with a full-sized snooker table as well as a poker table, and then opened the door beyond it. 'Sleeping quarters!'

Yes; because apparently it was sometimes easier to fall into the nearest bed rather than make the effort to go back to the castle and climb a flight of stairs. Or, if one had been his father or grandfather, one could smuggle the mistress of the moment in to stay there while their wives remained oblivious in the castle.

'Oh, this would've been a dream as a teenager. To be able to have a pool party-slash-sleepover here… What fun!'

Was that what she'd wished?

'Especially when one has a fully stocked kitchen at one's disposal,' she said when he led her through another doorway into the catering kitchen. 'This is industrial-sized!'

'And, given some of the parties that have taken place here, necessary.' He led her back out to the pool.

'Life in a castle is lived on a grander scale, huh?'

If one were his father and grandfather, absolutely.

'And yet here you are, rattling away on your own.'

'*Sì*, I am a poor little rich boy indeed, am I not?'

She rolled her eyes. 'My heart bleeds.'

He found himself fighting a smile. 'Besides, I'm not alone. You're here.'

'I don't count.'

He blinked. 'Why on earth not?'

'Because I'm a trespasser—uninvited and unwanted.'

'Sadie, I…'

'Oh, don't worry. I'm over our earlier spat. I'm here to do a job, that's all.' Shaking her head, she started walking beside the pool. 'I don't belong in this world.'

What on earth...?

'But it's fun to get a peek behind the curtain.'

She sent him a grin that momentarily knocked the air from his body. He took an involuntary step back. Why did her smile have that power? Was he still suffering the effects of the concussion? Had he locked himself away for too long? Maybe it was time to get back to work.

'And yet…'

He shook the troubling thoughts away to find her with her hands on her hips and her back to the pool as she surveyed the view again. 'And yet what?'

She waved a hand at the view. 'This pool house is extraordinary, but it's nothing on that.'

He imagined the expression on his father's and grandfather's faces if they'd heard her words and grinned.

'Oh!' She swung back, darted a glance at his leg. 'The pool must be great for therapy.'

He stiffened, his hands clenching around the cane. 'I don't *do therapy* here. I can manoeuvre the stairs down to the beach quite nicely, thank you.'

Not that he had. But she didn't need to know that.

'Oh, okay.' But then she sent him a comical hangdog look. 'Please don't make me go back down there now.'

His eyes narrowed. Did she doubt his ability, despite what he'd said?

'You might be used to negotiating the insane number of stairs in this place, but I'm not yet stair-fit. The trek up to the attics and then down to the beach have done me in.'

He had to laugh then, because she obviously meant it, and just like that everything was fine once more. He needed to stop being so touchy about his mobility. 'Then how about lunch instead?'

'Yes please.'

'And then we can investigate the treasure you brought down from the attic.'

'You're describing my perfect afternoon.'

Just as well. He had a lot to make up for.

Sadie halted when they reached the drawing room, setting the tan suitcase on top of a table. Enzo's lip curled. He loathed this room, filled as it was with memories of his father and grandfather—of shouting, smugness and casual cruelty.

He opened his mouth to suggest they move to the adjoining room when she said, 'The light's fabulous in here. Do you think we could…?'

She gestured to the table and then the bay windows. With a shrug, he'd helped her move it across to rest beneath them, where she'd get the full benefit of the natural light. He swore she held her breath as she unlatched the suitcase. It was more entertaining watching her face than seeing what she pulled forth.

She surveyed the lined-up treasures, lowering the suitcase to the floor. 'Your sister has a good eye.'

'Of course she does.' Chelsea was superior in every way.

'So let me explain what we have here.' She mentioned the names and brands of the teddy bear, clockwork robot, jack-in-the-box and toy dog. There were a couple of dolls and Dinky cars, and a spinning top too. 'Restored, these would be in huge demand on the open market. Some, like these two—' she indicated a Sweet Baby doll and a Barbie doll '—are vintage, but quite common, so they wouldn't fetch as much if you wanted to sell them.'

He didn't want to sell them. They were Chelsea's to do with as she pleased.

'How much would you charge to restore this lot?'

'I'm not charging you!'

'But—'

'Chelsea is my dearest friend in the world. While you...'

He found himself holding his breath.

'You, Enzo, have allowed me to storm your castle, and are letting me stay in this extraordinary place—' she gestured at the view '—to have the holiday of a lifetime.'

Her words had a funny lump lodging in his chest.

'It'll be an honour to restore these toys. A labour of love.'

'Noted,' he said, 'And greatly appreciated. But, for curiosity's sake, what would you normally charge?' *If* she had her own toy and doll hospital.

She cocked her head to one side. 'Well, let's see…' She touched each item lightly, making mental calculations, and then gave him a sum that had his brows lifting. 'I know it's expensive…'

'Nonsense! One should pay handsomely for your kind of expertise. I'm glad these things can be restored for Chelsea's children to enjoy. I'm glad you're making a living doing what you love.'

Her eyes went suspiciously bright. 'Thank you.'

Clearing his throat, he backed away, seeking an excuse to absent himself, to go and do something far away from her. Because a teasing, sassy Sadie was one thing, but a soft Sadie was an altogether different proposition. Instinct told him to retreat before he…what? He wasn't going to do *anything*.

A long-ago memory resurfaced, but he resolutely pushed it away. He definitely wasn't going to kiss her, and it would do no good to revisit that particular memory.

'Before you rush off…' Sadie dragged in a breath that had him halting. 'I'm under strict instructions from Chelsea to make sure it is in fact okay for her to take these things.'

'Of course it is!'

'Just so you know, this lot is worth a small fortune.'

She named a sum that had his eyes widening. 'Toys are worth that much?'

'These ones are. And, while we're on the topic of money, that's a vintage Goyard suitcase there and worth at least two thousand euros.'

He shook himself. 'Whatever these things are worth, Sadie, I want Chelsea to have them. She'll cherish them, and her children will cherish them, and that's as it should be.' He shifted and frowned. 'She wanted you to make sure...?'

'She'd rather die than have you thinking she was taking advantage of you.'

'She—?'

'I know, I know! I told her you'd never think that, but she's seen plenty of other people take advantage of you, and she's determined to never do anything that will make you feel like that.'

Would it really be so bad to have a party?

Rolling his shoulders, he shook off the thought. He wasn't having a party, but... 'I'll ring her.'

Striding away, he pulled his phone from his pocket and dialled. Since Chelsea had moved to Europe last year, he no longer had to calculate the time difference.

'Enzo!' Chelsea's voice and the excitement in it reached him down the line, making him smile. 'It's great to hear from you! How are you?'

'Very well. The toys you want are apparently worth a small fortune.'

'Oh, God—'

'But I do not care. They are yours, and I don't want to hear any arguments.'

They talked for a little while and laughed. He should've taken the initiative to ring her sooner. He should ring his mother too.

'Enzo, can I ask you a favour?'

His stomach screwed up tightly. He *didn't* want a party. 'You can ask.'

Chelsea laughed. 'Hedging your bets, huh? I don't think it's a huge favour. It's just…can you make sure that Sadie doesn't bury herself in the attics for the entire fortnight?'

He bit back a sigh. 'I will do my best.' But it wasn't any of his business how Sadie wanted to spend her time.

'It's just…'

His every sense went on high alert at the sudden strain in her voice. 'Yes?'

'She'd probably kill me for telling you.'

'Not literally. Go on.'

'Well, Sadie's recently had some unsettling news. Her…um…her mother has returned.'

What the hell? Sadie's mother had abandoned her as a baby and left her to be raised by her grandparents. And now she was home…

He forked a hand through his hair. Chelsea and Sadie had become the best of best friends at boarding school in Australia. His stepfather

Stephen was Australian and had travelled a lot for work. It was how he'd met Enzo's mother. After his first wife's death, he'd sent his daughter to the very best schools.

Sadie's background had been very different. She'd been one of a handful of scholarship students—awarded full board and tuition due to academic excellence. Chelsea had felt cast adrift at boarding school and had been still grieving the death of her mother. Sadie had…

He swallowed. As Chelsea told it, Sadie had saved her, had made her feel less alone, and had made her laugh again. Sadie had made her see the future could be a happy place.

She taught me to dream again.

That was why Sadie had always been off-limits to him. Because she meant as much to Chelsea as the rest of their family did. If he ever did anything to hurt Sadie, Chelsea would never forgive him. It could create the ugliest of splits, which would break his mother's heart, and he couldn't bear that thought.

But Sadie's mother had come home… 'Has Sadie actually seen her?'

'Yes. It didn't go well.'

'So you sent her here?'

'Two birds, one stone,' she whispered. 'I really do want those toys restored and I knew that would be something she'd love to do. I hope you don't mind me imposing like this, Enzo.'

'No, it was a good thing to do.' Sadie's mother

had come home… As he rang off, he found he didn't mind Chelsea sending Sadie here. Not now. Not one little bit.

CHAPTER FOUR

SADIE DIDN'T SEE Enzo until dinner time. No doubt he was avoiding her which, God forbid, suited her just fine. They both needed a time-out after that ugly spat. Some people could take that kind of thing in their stride, but she wasn't one of them. She suspected Enzo wasn't either.

Funny, but she hadn't grown up with anyone yelling at her as a child. Her grandparents were gentle people, kind enough in their own way, though joyfulness hadn't featured large in their lives. If she was being bluntly honest, joy hadn't featured in their lives at all.

Until recently. And that had only brought home to her how short she'd always fallen in their affections. It was hard to love someone with her whole heart only to have them not love her back in equal measure or even a half measure. That was the way to a broken heart. It wasn't just some gorgeous guy who promised someone the world and then ran away at the first sign of trouble who could break one's heart. One's family and friends could break it too. And it was almost a relief to realise that after so long.

Which was why, from now on, she would wrap her heart in bubble wrap, cotton wool and shock-absorbent rubber and place it in a big, steel box with a whopping great padlock. She hadn't been enough for her mother. She hadn't been enough for her grandparents. And, other than Chelsea, she hadn't been enough for the girls at the boarding school either. Nine years ago, she hadn't been enough for Enzo. She wouldn't let anyone else make her feel 'not enough'.

The guys you've dated over the years haven't been like that.

She'd mostly dated nice guys. None of them had set her world on fire, though. She'd not been able to envisage a future with any of them. Maybe at some indefinable point in the future she'd meet someone who would change her mind. But love wasn't on the agenda for the immediate future. Creating a life she loved needed to be her top priority. A life with strong foundations. A life that wouldn't let her down.

'Are you still going over what happened earlier?'

Enzo stood in the doorway of the dining room, surveying her with those dark eyes of his, and she sent him a swift smile. 'Nope, just off with the fairies.'

'They're bad fairies, then.' He took a seat. 'Are you sure I don't need to apologise again?'

'Positive. Besides…' she grinned '… I think you've had enough practice for one day. I was just reflecting on the fact…' Gah! What was she doing? She was supposed to be bright, breezy and *insouciant*—not earnest and serious.

'Yes?' That raised eyebrow assured her she wouldn't get away without an explanation, and what the heck? The truth was better than making things awkward between them again.

'You were reflecting on…?'

Luisa entered with their plates. Sadie stared at the vision of tuna on a bed of finely sliced crispy potatoes and the side of buttered steamed vegetables that were placed in front of her. She lifted amazed eyes to the other woman.

Luisa winked. *'Bon appétit.'*

'This looks like heaven.' Seizing her cutlery, Sadie pointed her fork in the direction in which the housekeeper had disappeared. 'She's wonderful.'

'Agreed. As you were saying…?'

She laughed. She could manage some teasing mixed in with the seriousness. 'Never fear, I will reveal all. I just have to try the tuna first.'

She did, and it was perfection. Closing her eyes, she relished the taste and texture. This was her favourite meal. When she opened them again, she found Enzo gazing at her with the same expression he'd had in his eyes when she'd examined Chelsea's selection of toys. Her mouth went dry. It was the same expression he'd worn the night he'd kissed her when she'd been eighteen—heated, hungry, wolfish.

An answering heat unfurled deep inside her but, unlike nine years ago, she knew this sensation was lust, not love. She knew the difference now and maybe…

Oh, God. Do not be tempted!

Dragging her gaze away, she did her best to quench the heat with two undeniable facts. The first was that Enzo didn't want to feel that heat; she could tell he resented it. The second was the fact he was nursing a broken heart. She had no desire to be anyone's rebound fling. She was worth more than that.

Oh, and there was a third reason for good measure: she would never be enough for Enzo. Ever. And she was through with all that. Enzo came from a completely different world and, as his mother had once pointed out, she would never fit into it. She didn't have the resources to deal with more failure at the moment. She'd left her family; had quit her job. She was moving to Europe to start a new life. *That* was enough.

She glanced across to find Enzo raising an impatient eyebrow that had her wanting to pelt him with the warmed bread rolls. 'You were reflecting on…?'

'Patience isn't your strong suit, is it?'

He blinked.

'And, now that my reflections have been built up to a fever pitch of expectation, you're going to find them terribly anticlimactic. I was merely pondering the fact that you'd deliberately kept your distance this afternoon, and that I was glad of it. It gave us both a chance to regroup.' She shrugged. 'Which in turn had me reflecting on the fact that neither of us are the kind of people who can easily shrug off a shouting match.'

His lips twisted. 'From memory, you didn't do any of the shouting.'

'Regardless, it's still not a "water off a duck's back" thing for us.' She sliced into her tuna. 'Don't you think it's strange when we've had such different upbringings? My grandparents never shouted at me. Occasionally the teachers at boarding school would raise their voices, but no one yelled at us in "sergeant major" fashion.'

The other girls hadn't shouted at Sadie either. Their spite had arrived in quieter and crueller ways.

'Whereas you had a very different experience. Your father and grandfather lost their tempers on a regular basis.' Part of her grieved for the small boy who'd had to bear all that anger.

'*Sì.* A week rarely passed without a temper tantrum from one of them. All of that drama is exhausting. That's why such behaviour now is anathema to me.' He hesitated. 'It's one of the reasons my behaviour this morning appalled me. Theirs is not an example I wish to emulate.'

The tuna promptly lost its flavour. Sadie swallowed her current mouthful, and it settled in her stomach like a lead weight. 'Enzo, you're *nothing* like them.'

'Actions speak louder than words.'

She slammed down her cutlery. 'Five months ago you went through an extraordinarily traumatic event. Then you holed yourself up here in your castle without anyone to talk to. That's a recipe for volcanic outbursts, not an indication you've inherited genetic character flaws. Your father and grandfather were selfish men, but you're not.' She wished he'd look at her. 'But that doesn't mean you're not allowed to be angry sometimes. That's impossible for anyone.'

'The way I choose to unleash that anger is entirely my responsibility.'

She doubted he'd had much choice. The anger and frustration must have built and built until it had taken him entirely off-guard. He'd just…exploded. And, while she might've found it confronting, she hadn't feared for her safety. It had still been Enzo shouting, and Enzo wouldn't hurt any woman. It had probably done him the world of good to get some of that out of his system.

'Anyone would feel angry in your shoes. There was no rhyme or reason for your accident.'

His gaze snapped away and something in her chest faltered. There hadn't been a reason…had there? According to Chelsea, Enzo couldn't remember the crash. The accident had occurred on a particularly dangerous piece of road. The authorities had said it was lucky the car hadn't gone over the cliff—a thought that chilled her to the bone.

Not remembering must plague him. Claudia's injuries hadn't been as severe, but she'd been dozing at the time, and hadn't been able to shed light on what had happened. Knowing Enzo, he probably felt responsible for her injuries too.

Chelsea's scathing critique of Claudia's abandonment of Enzo in his hour of need went round and round in her mind now and she wanted to bury her face in the snowy white linen of her napkin. Had Enzo's scars really appalled the other woman so much? How could she be so insensitive, so heartless?

Sadie had noticed his pallor when she had mentioned her name…

Don't think about that now.

'You've had to endure a great deal of pain, and the frustration of a slow recovery—and you're not a naturally indolent guy—so that's been a challenge in itself.'

Those disturbing lips twitched. 'Is that a polite way of calling me impatient?'

'I wouldn't dream of calling you any such thing!'

He huffed out a laugh. 'If I recall correctly, that's exactly what you just called me.'

The tension in her chest eased a fraction. 'All I'm saying is you've suffered a terrible accident that's turned your whole life on its head. In your place, anyone would feel angry.'

'That doesn't excuse my earlier behaviour.'

'Look, Enzo, you've apologised and I've accepted your apology. Will you please stop wallowing?'

He choked on a spear of asparagus. 'You really aren't a gently-gently person any more, are you, Sadie?'

'Oh, if I were dispensing with the gently-gently approach…' She rested her chin in her hand. 'Has it not occurred to you that your outburst might in fact be an indication that the way you've been dealing with your situation isn't in fact the best way?'

His eyes immediately narrowed into a glare. She did her best to shrug *insouciantly*. 'I understand the urge to bury yourself away from prying eyes, but surely that has an end date?'

'Does it?' Dark eyes skewered her to her seat. 'Are you here to provide me with therapy, Sadie? Is that the role you see for yourself?'

Oh, and there was the anger lurking just beneath the surface. 'Afraid I'm not qualified.' She held his gaze. 'Do *you* think you need to see a therapist?' When he remained silent, she added, 'Or do you just need to stop feeling sorry for yourself?'

It was entirely possible she'd gone too far, but for some reason she was starting to feel angry herself, so she didn't care. 'Self-pity *is* an emotion I've a lot of experience with, though. I spent all of my teenage years in a haze of "woe is me".'

'Nonsense!' he growled, throwing his napkin down beside his plate. 'You never came across as self-pitying.'

'Guess I hid it well.'

Crossing his arms, he raised an eyebrow. 'Why did you feel sorry for yourself?'

She shrugged. 'The girls at school made it clear I was an outsider—that I wasn't one of them.'

At the age of twelve, Sadie had won a full scholarship to a prestigious girls' boarding school in rural Victoria—five hours from Melbourne. She'd been so excited and so quietly proud of herself.

And then had come the reality.

Her grandparents were solid, working-class people—her grandmother a housewife and Pop a train driver. The other girls at school, though, had been the daughters of pastoralists, industrialists, politicians, vice chancellors of universities, High Court judges—the crème de la crème of Australian society.

Some of them had been the progeny of single mothers—not all had come from happy homes—but nobody else's mother had dumped them with their grandparents as a baby and ridden off in the sunset, never to be heard from again. When the girls from school had found that out they'd dubbed Sadie 'UP': the unidentified package at the baggage claim; lost property.

Pushing away the remembered misery, she lifted her chin. 'I didn't fit in anywhere. If Chelsea hadn't told them to back off before claiming me for her BFF, I don't know what I would've done.'

Enzo stared at her with something like horror. For a horrible moment she wanted to hide from all she'd revealed. 'No matter how much I wanted to go back to my old school, I had to stick it out, because my grandparents were overjoyed to no longer have the day-to-day care of me.'

He started. 'Oh, come, Sadie. That has to be an exaggeration.'

'Of course it is.' She winked at him, aiming for levity again. 'As my grandparents don't do joy, they couldn't do *over*joyed, right?'

He snorted. 'Not what I meant.'

'I was a teenager, Enzo. Hyperbole was my default setting. And, while I know my grandparents must love me in their own way, they shouldn't have been lumped with me in the first place. So, while overjoyed is an exaggeration, their poorly disguised relief was not.'

Even now that knowledge had the power to wound her. She'd always been a duty to them rather than a source of pleasure or delight. They'd never been unreasonable, they'd never been unkind, but beneath their kindness had been weariness and sadness. They'd missed her mother. They'd *wanted* her mother. Sadie hadn't even reached the heights of being a poor substitute.

'So, to my mind, I wasn't wanted at school, I

wasn't wanted at home…and don't get me started on my mother.'

He stared at her for two beats. 'None of this was obvious on your holidays with us.'

From the ages of thirteen to eighteen, she'd spent several weeks over the summer with Chelsea and her family at their mansion on the Mornington Peninsula, with its spectacular views of the rugged coastline. Their kind of wealth had been previously unknown to her. There'd been a huge swimming pool, tennis courts and an extraordinary games room. They'd swum, gone for long walks and had simply hung out. Those summers had afforded her the time simply to be—nothing had been asked of her, nothing demanded, except that she have fun. Chelsea's family had been every bit as kind and warm as Chelsea herself. It had all felt so magical.

'Those holidays were my respite, a chance to breathe freely. I swear they gave me the strength to deal with the rest of the year.'

'So how did you manage to drag yourself out of this miasma of self-pity?'

'Started focusing on the things I did have. I had a best friend, and that's no small thing. I buried myself in the things I loved as much as I could—big, fat fantasy novels and fixing things.'

'Like broken toys.'

'I have a knack for it.'

His brow puckered. 'How? Why?'

'Ah, well, that's down to Mrs Aberglasslyn—

my grandparents' next-door neighbour. She owned a doll hospital and restored all manner of toys. I was probably six the first time I snuck over to peep inside her workshop.' She'd thought it a wonderland. 'Rather than chase me away, she welcomed me in and showed me what she was working on.'

She smiled at the memory. 'We became firm friends and over the years Ada taught me all that she knew.' A decade older than Sadie's mother, Ada had been the other godsend in Sadie's life. In her late sixties now, she'd retired to the coast. Sadie visited from time to time.

She glanced back at Enzo, who'd remained quiet for too long. 'I told myself that saying, that this too would pass. I knew that one day I'd be an adult and then I could shape my life however I wanted.' Had she, though? Or had she fallen into patterns that wouldn't create waves because that was what she was used to doing? Such as not pursuing her dream to open her toy repair shop, which she also thought of affectionately as a doll hospital, as that was her speciality.

Enzo remained deep in thought and she pushed her own disturbing thoughts away to reapply herself to her meal.

'So…' Enzo glared at his plate. 'This party idea that Chelsea has concocted—it's supposed to force me out of the doldrums?'

Carefully finishing her food, Sadie reached for her napkin and dabbed her mouth. 'I wish a party could make you feel like your old self again…'

She shook her head. 'But the party isn't for you, not really, though I don't think Chelsea realises that.'

'What are you talking about?'

'The party is for your family, Enzo. So they can assure themselves that you are in fact okay and on the road to recovery.'

She waited for him to swear, to explode. He did neither. He did pale, though, and she berated herself for her bluntness.

Dragging in a breath that made his nostrils flare, he shook his head. 'Can we change the subject?'

'Excellent idea.' She was supposed to be cheering him up—not making the doldrums even more doldrum-y!

The party isn't for you... The party is for your family. The unalloyed truth of Sadie's words sank into Enzo's bones. Maybe it would be selfish of him to deny them this party, but to have to be cheerful, to put on a show to put their minds at rest… The thought exhausted him. He'd have to field questions—questions that until now they'd refrained from asking.

When will you go back to work?

Do you plan to return to Milan?

Are you starting to feel better?

He didn't know the answers to any of those questions. And there were other questions he dreaded even more.

Have you remembered anything about the accident?

Have you spoken to Claudia?

Lying about the accident didn't sit well with him, but telling the truth was unthinkable.

Fact was, it wouldn't just be a party. It'd be a thinly veiled inquisition. And maybe right now wasn't the best time to consider the pros and cons of a party, when his leg was aching from his exercises and the unaccustomed activity, and his mind was aching from the discovery of how alone Sadie had felt growing up—and the fact her mother had returned.

Sadie clapped her hands. 'After dinner, why don't I grab that box of stuff I brought down from the attic and you can open the jewellery box and vanity case?'

'You haven't gone through it yet?'

'They're *your* things, Enzo. I couldn't do it without you, even though I'm dying to see what we'll find.'

'You've my permission.'

'I opened the suitcase. It's only fair you share the thrill of discovery. Gird your loins, though, it could all end in disappointment. But it's still exciting, don't you think?'

He scratched a hand through his hair. When was the last time anything had *properly* excited him? Did getting out of hospital count? Before that…he couldn't remember.

Sadie took his silence as acquiescence, which

was how he found himself standing at the little dining table after dinner, in front of the bank of windows in the detested drawing room with the jewellery box in front of him. Sadie shook out a piece of black velvet from her work bag and spread it beside the box. Folding her arms, she stepped back and simply waited.

Strangely, he found he didn't mind. In fact, maybe even the thinnest thread of anticipation lifted through him, even though he knew nothing of value would be inside—his father and grandfather had sold the family jewels and expensive artworks long ago.

He lifted the lid…to reveal a beautiful, ornate necklace. Lifting it out, he set it on Sadie's piece of velvet, along with a matching brooch and earrings.

'I know a "man of quality" should be able to recognise real diamonds when he sees them, but I haven't a clue.' He couldn't stop his lip from curling. 'As my father knew quality, though, it leads me to suppose these are mere replicas.'

She snorted. 'Your father knew diddly squat.'

He bit back a grin. 'He could tell a genuine diamond from twenty paces.'

'What your father saw were dollar signs. He didn't see beauty.'

Her words made him still.

Reaching for an eyepiece, she bent down to study the necklace. Her dark hair caught the setting sun and for a brief moment it gleamed like walnut silk. 'These pieces might be paste, but they're undeniably beautiful.'

He dragged his gaze from a face alive with animation, and also undeniably beautiful, and swallowed. *'Sì.'*

'Also, it's an exemplary specimen of paste jewellery and I'd date it from the mid-1800s.'

'So this is...?'

She straightened. 'Nearly two hundred years old. What your idiot father couldn't see is that this piece would fetch thousands at auction.'

He smiled at the casual way she hurled insults at his father, but also at the knowledge this piece had bested the older man. 'I don't think I'll sell it.'

'No, it's probably freighted with family history.'

Which promptly made it lose some of its glitter. His family history was nothing to be proud of.

'I bet there's an interesting back story.'

Probably 'interesting' as in awful, he thought, but he left that unsaid. He didn't want to diminish the sparkle in her eyes or her enjoyment in their treasure hunt.

She gestured to the box again. 'What else is hiding in there?'

He opened the two drawers, but they were empty. 'Looks like that's it.'

She frowned. 'May I?'

He immediately stepped aside and gestured for her to take his place. She hefted the box in her hands, as if assessing its weight. Setting it back down, she ran a hand across it slowly, and then stilled. Glancing up at him, she gave a silent scream. 'Give me your hand.'

He did and immediately felt the warmth of her hand, the softness of her skin.

'Feel that?'

His attention snapped back as she ran his finger over a slight depression in the wood. 'I…yes.'

She moved her hand from his to clasp both hands beneath her chin, practically dancing on the spot. The warmth of her hand lingered and that cute smile had heat gathering beneath his breast bone. Damn it! Sadie Beckett was adorable. When had that happened?

She's always been adorable.

'What are you waiting for, Enzo? Press it!'

He couldn't help laughing at her impatience, but that thread of earlier anticipation had grown thick enough now to knit into a sweater. He depressed the button and a secret compartment sprang open to reveal a man's yellow-gold pocket watch. Lifting it out, he set it gently on the velvet beside the paste necklace.

They both bent over it, their heads nearly touching, and her scent filled his senses—something fresh, floral and utterly enlivening. The air whistled between Sadie's teeth. She glanced across at him. 'Now *this* is a find. It's…'

Her words stumbled to a halt and those hazel eyes blinked, as if surprised to find she and Enzo had drawn so close. But then, oh, so slowly, they drifted down to his lips, the gold in their depths sparking. His gaze lowered to her lips—plump, soft, inviting—and heat gathered in his veins, snapping parts of him alive with a fierce hunger. It'd be so easy to…

Sadie snapped upright. Her gaze jerked back to the watch, but a pulse pounded in her throat, betraying her agitation. He stepped back and the sheer difficulty of it had him breathing heavily. While Sadie hadn't flinched at his scars, that didn't mean she wanted him near her. It didn't mean she wanted him to kiss her. And, if he did kiss her, there was every chance she'd only kiss him back out of pity.

That thought doused him as affectively as an ice-cold jet of water. He was careful not to direct any of his anger and loathing at her, though. It was time to stop lashing out like an angry animal. He might find her captivating, and the thought of losing himself to pleasure for a short time held a seductive power that shocked him. But when he'd been lying in a hospital bed, reeling at all Claudia had done, he'd sworn he was done with relationships; with thinking he might one day find the kind of love his mother had found with Stephen. It wasn't worth the risk.

He attracted women who were reasonable and kind on the surface, but who, when they couldn't mould him into what they wanted, threw the kind of temper tantrums that made his blood run cold. He'd had to deal with outbursts, fits of pique, sulking and dreadful insults. He'd had flowers and jewellery thrown at him.

And then there'd been Claudia. Enough was enough. He'd rather be alone than replicate the kind of relationship his parents had shared.

Pulling himself into tight straight lines, he gestured at the watch. 'Treasure?'

'Yes.'

She'd immersed herself in examining the watch again, as if that fraught moment was already forgotten. He rolled his shoulders and fought a frown.

'This is rare—an antique LeCoultre; Swiss. Highly sought after, if in working order, and worth a lot of money.'

Someone had hidden this watch, probably from the thieving greed of the likes of his father, which inclined him favourably towards it. 'Does it work?'

She wound it, and they held their breaths…but nothing happened.

'I'd love to try and fix it.'

'Feel free.'

She sent him her 'school ma'am' look. 'You're far too free with your things.'

'They're just things. Have you ever fixed an antique watch?'

'Sure, but—'

'There you go, you're the expert.' He took the watch, relishing the weight and heft of it. The gold warmed in his hand, and fitted there as if it belonged. 'It'd be nice to see this working.'

When he turned it over, Sadie pointed. 'Who's "Felix"?'

He searched his memory banks, but came back blank. 'My grandfather schooled me on the names of my forbears.' He'd insisted Enzo learn to recite them at the age of twelve. And he had enforced his decree with a heavy leather strap until Enzo could recite his Lombardi lineage perfectly. 'I've no recollection of a Felix.'

Acid burned his stomach. Behind their cultured façade, the Lombardis had been nothing but a bunch of raping, pillaging thugs.

'Maybe these will give us a clue.' She gestured to the box. 'It's filled with old diaries.' She gave one of those excited shimmies. 'Aren't you eager to dip inside them and learn what your relations were really like?'

He knew enough already. But he refused to spoil her fun. *Her mother has returned.* He could only imagine how that had turned Sadie's world on its head. If he could provide her with a distraction or ten for the next fortnight, he would.

'Nope, but knock yourself out.' He pointed to the vanity case. 'I already know what's in that.'

Her eyes brightened. 'What?'

'Take a look.'

As expected, her eyes lit up when she sifted through his grandmother's collection of scent bottles. 'So pretty,' she sighed. 'You should have these on display somewhere.'

'If you find somewhere appropriate, then feel free.' The memories he had of his grandmother, at least, were dear to him.

Sadie turned back, eyes wide and lips parted, which had things clenching up inside him he didn't want. Turning on his heel, he moved into the adjacent room and sat down in his battered arm chair. If she wanted to interpret that as him needing to rest, so be it. It would be preferable to the truth—that he needed the distance.

She followed him and he raised an eyebrow. 'Now, tell me what you'd like to do this evening.'

She sat on the edge of the sofa and nibbled her bottom lip. 'Well, I couldn't help noticing you have an excellent DVD collection, including a bunch of old films I've never seen before. And I was wondering…'

He could watch a film with her and then excuse himself for the evening. It'd be low key, with little asked of him but it'd provide a big tick in the 'good host' column. 'Choose your poison.' Seizing the remote, he pointed it to the big-screen TV.

She rubbed her hands together. 'Audrey Hepburn and *My Fair Lady*, here we come. I'm in the mood for comedy—a lot of comedy—and it's supposed to be fun.'

Which sounded good to him. Sadie was probably in dire need of light-hearted fun. That was tonight taken care of. Now for tomorrow…

'How's this for a plan—tomorrow we have a session in the attic for an hour or two, before heading down to the beach for a swim?'

She stared at him as if he'd given her the moon. He had to fight an urge to puff out his chest.

'Sì.' He nodded. 'That looks as if it meets with your approval. And then, if you wish to return to the attics in the afternoon, you can do so.'

'It sounds like heaven, Enzo.'

No, it didn't. But it was the best that he could manage in the circumstances.

CHAPTER FIVE

SADIE OPENED THE attic door the following morning and stepped inside. Chelsea had sent her photos, of course, but they hadn't prepared her for the reality of standing here amid the Lombardi family's toy collection.

'Oh, Enzo.' She clasped her hands beneath her chin and reminded herself to keep breathing. 'This is *amazing*!'

Even with her attention glued to the scene in front of them, Sadie was aware that Enzo stared at her with a mixture of bemusement, amusement and a touch of impatience…spiced with a hint of affection. Which seemed a lot of reaction to take in, when ninety percent of her attention remained firmly glued to the collection.

Why hasn't it all *your attention? This collection is a once-in-a-lifetime find!*

She rolled her shoulders. *Shut up.* Enzo had always been impossible to ignore. And, even though she no longer had a crush on him, no longer harboured any silly girlish dreams involving knights and white horses, he was still the main reason she was here.

Instead of focussing minutely on Enzo, she made herself take preliminary stock of the room. A central aisle ran down its length, while display cabinets branched off to form horizontal rows either side.

She started down its length. 'This is extraordinary. Not just a collection, but a *museum*.'

'You haven't examined anything yet. You can't…'

But Sadie had stopped listening. She halted. Her hand lifted to wrap around the ridiculously firm flesh of Enzo's forearm to drag him to a stop too. She stared at the item beneath the dormer window at the end of the row and her heart expanded. Forcing her fingers to release him, she sashayed down the aisle towards it. *'Hubba hubba!'*

'Did you just say…?'

'Enzo, meet the object of all my dreams, the true hero of my heart.' She gestured to the wooden rocking horse that stood there in solitary nobility, before kneeling down in front of it.

'The hero of your heart is… *Black Beauty?*'

She stroked a reverential finger down the horse's nose and touched its mane. 'Except this one is a dapple grey.' And it was in the most excellent condition.

'I thought Mr Darcy—'

'The perfect name!' She beamed up at him

from where she kneeled. 'Enzo, meet Mr Darcy. Mr Darcy, Enzo.'

He rolled his eyes. 'Sadie…'

'I fell in love with a guy not too dissimilar to this one when I was seven years old.'

She watched Enzo rest his back against the display case behind him, moving his walking stick from his right hand to his left. Was his leg giving him gyp?

'Did you?'

How would he make it down the steep path to the beach when his leg already hurt?

'Sadie?'

She shook herself. 'He was in the window of a barber's shop, of all places, and it was love at first sight. I begged my grandmother to let us take him home.' She'd never been a child who asked for much, but she'd wanted that rocking horse so fiercely, she'd cried. She could still remember the scolding she'd received. She'd hadn't asked for anything that had really mattered since, until last month.

'I take it you were met with a stern refusal.'

'Of course.' She worked hard to keep her voice light. 'I don't even know if it was for sale. And, as I was only seven, I had no notion how expensive these guys could be.' She pressed her hands to her heart. 'Hence began a lifetime of unrequited love.'

She rolled her eyes. Unrequited love seemed to be the theme of her life. *Not any more.* She very gently moved the horse on its glider mechanism. It moved smoothly, as if someone had taken great pains to oil it over the years.

'In your line of work, you must've come across other such specimens?'

'A couple.' She rose to examine the saddle and stirrups. 'But none of those were for sale either.' The tail was as thick and lush as the mane and, while the paint had faded over the years, it wouldn't take much to bring this guy back to mint condition.

She stepped back, hands on hips. 'This fellow is in excellent condition, Enzo. He's beautiful.'

'If you want him, Sadie, he's yours.'

He said it so easily, as if it was nothing. She jerked round. 'No! You can't do that.'

'He's mine. I can do what I please with him.'

Enzo was extraordinarily generous, but she shook her head. 'Mr Darcy wouldn't be happy in my pokey little flat.' The pokey little flat she'd packed up and no longer rented—not that she'd told anybody that yet. 'Think how happy he must be here, with all this room to run around in.'

A rather delicious frown settled on his brow. 'I don't know if you've noticed, but Mr Darcy is an inanimate toy.'

'But don't you think it's fun to imagine all these toys coming to life when we're not watching, and having lives and adventures of their own?'

His mouth opened; he closed it again and frowned.

'Well, I do.' She led him back to the central aisle. 'And you're not going to rain on my parade.'

'Wouldn't dream of it.'

'Gallantly said!'

He really was making an effort. She sent him a grin and he blinked, as if it had taken him off-guard. Given her bossy brassiness of the previous day—and she still couldn't think of that without wincing—he probably was. They were both trying their best to be normal reasonable people. *Go us!*

She sensed he wanted to press the matter of the rocking horse, but when he opened his mouth, she leapt in first. 'I didn't come here to profit from you, either financially or materially, and it would offend me deeply to do so. I will not break up your collection, Enzo.'

His frown deepened. She frowned back playfully until a smile tugged at his lips. He might not think it at the moment with his broken heart—the thought of which had her own chest growing heavy—but one day he might have a little girl who'd fall in love with that rocking horse as deeply as she once had with the horse in the barber's shop. He'd be glad he still had Mr Darcy then.

They chose to browse different rows. The Lombardi collection was surprisingly eclectic, with toys from the 1980s sitting side by side with toys over a hundred years older. They eventually met back in the central aisle.

Folding her arms, Sadie turned on the spot. 'I don't think I'll manage to catalogue the entire collection in a fortnight.' Not if she was also doing all she could to cheer him up and get him out in the sun…where hopefully she could eventually talk him into the party Chelsea had her heart set on hosting. She wrinkled her nose in apology—whether for not being able to fully catalogue his collection, or because she intended to keep hassling him about the party, she couldn't say. 'I expect it will just be edited highlights.'

'You don't need to catalogue anything.'

'But I want to. You don't understand what a treat this is.' Besides, it would be handy for him to have.

He set his cane in front of him, rested both hands on it and bent slightly at the waist. His eyes were a deep, dark brown, and they had a slightly lighter halo around the pupil that fascinated her. It took all her strength not to lean in closer to get a better look.

'Why?'

She blinked. 'Pardon?'

'You said you didn't want to profit financially or materially. So why are you going to so much trouble for Chelsea…and for me?'

Oh.

He continued. 'Chelsea has this hare-brained scheme to throw me a surprise birthday party—something you clearly have reservations about as you *haven't* kept it a secret, and yet you're still rushing to do her bidding.'

He made her sound like a lackey or minion, when nothing could be further from the truth. 'There's no single simple answer to that.' She glanced at her watch. As suspected, she'd kept him up here long enough. 'I'm happy to attempt an answer, but maybe it's time to head down to the beach.' She glanced at the way his knuckles had whitened around his walking stick. 'Or perhaps the pool for a few lazy laps.'

His eyes narrowed. 'You don't think I can manage the path?'

'I've no idea; but, before you bite my head off, two things…' She held up two fingers. 'First, I don't want to be responsible for anything that might delay or inhibit your recovery. Second, are you the kind of guy who would recklessly race down that hill just to prove to some girl he doesn't give two hoots about that he's manly enough to do it?'

He eased back and blinked. 'I give two hoots about you, Sadie. You're a family friend.'

Her stomach scrunched up into a tight ball. *Ouch!* Enzo would never see her as anything more than his little sister's best friend, would he? He probably didn't even see her as a woman.

Do you want to explain those smouldering looks he's been sending you?

She rolled her shoulders. They didn't mean anything, not really. Enzo was mad at the world.

The way Claudia had abandoned him had left his pride in tatters. It was only natural he'd want to reassure himself that women could still find him attractive.

She didn't care if he saw her as a woman or not. She wasn't going to resurrect that stupid crush she'd had on him. Nor was she going to let him shore up his male pride at her expense.

She folded her arms. 'I'm just saying that, if this is some male pride thing, then I want no part of it. I refuse to be responsible for you injuring yourself more. I'll just stay up here and do my lazy laps in the pool.'

His jaw worked; eventually he said, 'Would it make a difference if I told you I'd spoken to my doctor yesterday and he gave me the all-clear—on the proviso I take it slowly and rest at both ends?'

'Did you?'

'I might be proud, Sadie, but I'm not foolish. I've no wish to hinder my recovery. Shall we meet on the terrace in twenty minutes?'

She met him on the terrace a quarter of an hour later. He refused to relinquish the bag slung over one shoulder, gesturing for her to precede him along the path.

'If you stumble, I'll break your fall,' she chirped over her shoulder. 'Your own personal human-sized airbag.'

'Windbag, I think you mean.'

She snorted. *Look at him, being all teasing and relaxed, and the complete opposite of the grumpy bear from yesterday.*

She took the path slowly, but there was no denying the strain around Enzo's mouth when they finally reached the beach. She wordlessly took the beach bag from him and laid their towels out on the strip of golden sand. Once he'd seated himself, she handed him a water bottle and fished out the painkillers Luisa had handed her before they'd left.

He hesitated and then took one. She didn't say anything, and didn't tell him he'd done a good job. She feared anything she said would sound patronising. She also suspected that the difficulty of the descent had shocked him, and she had no desire to make him feel any more self-conscious.

Instead, she settled on her towel, drank deeply from the other water bottle—and drank in the view. 'Lord, Enzo, you're living in paradise.' Did he plan to make the castle his permanent home? She would in a heartbeat, if it were hers.

'Don't wait for me, Sadie. Go do your lazy laps, as I know you're dying to.'

'Ha! What you're really saying is, I look like I need cooling off. My face is bright-red, isn't it?'

Those stern lips twitched a little. 'Beneath the glow, you're still pale. A bit of sun will do you good.'

The water did look inviting. 'Aren't you coming in?'

His face immediately shuttered. 'No.'

Why not?

He closed his eyes, as if to shut her and the sight of the water out. Maybe he wanted a quiet moment to himself first, without her hovering. She'd hate that too; it set her teeth on edge. She didn't want to set Enzo's teeth on edge any more than she already had.

Leaping to her feet, she seized the hem of her T-shirt and pulled it over her head. 'If you're happy to wait for my answer to your earlier question, then…'

Dark eyes sprang open again. 'Actually, I'd like to hear your answer. I thought you were avoiding the question. I didn't want to press.'

His eyes widened when he realised she'd halted with her shirt halfway between waist and chin, leaving her midriff bare. Those compelling eyes darkened and travelled over her with a lazy thoroughness that had her skin sparking with instant heat. In this moment, Enzo *definitely* saw her a woman.

Her heart pounded in her ears and she tried not to groan, swoon or melt. She mightn't have a teenage crush on Enzo Lombardi any more, but there was no denying the man was darkly attractive, utterly compelling and smoking hot. Or the fact that she wanted him with every atom of her now very *adult* female body…

Enzo wanted to blame the exertion of the walk and a restless night for the barriers he felt dissolving between his beguiling house guest and him. But, despite wishing otherwise, if he was honest he found Sadie far too tempting with her lush, pursed lips, her glossy dark hair and those dancing hazel eyes. He had since the night of the summer ball nine years ago, when he'd kissed her.

Damn it, she was Chelsea's best friend. Even if she wasn't off-limits due to that unspoken code, he wasn't interested in pursuing any kind of romantic entanglement. Everything that had happened with Claudia was still too fresh in his mind.

Then stop staring at her as if you'd like to ravish her.

Except, somehow, that was impossible. Their gazes remained locked in some kind of silent battle—as if neither of them could look away. Her lips parted and a breath shuddered out of her. He was seized with a desperate urge to leap to his feet, pull her into his arms and kiss her until neither one of them could think straight. She stared at him as if that was exactly what she wanted too.

He remembered the taste of her—it had been sweet and addictive. He hungered for just the briefest taste again now…

Leap—you? With that leg of yours?

Swallowing a curse, he dragged his gaze away and slammed his sunglasses onto his face. He stared at the water, which was still, smooth and reflected back the perfect blue of the sky like a summer promise. In his chest, though, his heart dashed itself against storm-tossed rocks.

You'd probably fall flat on your face.

He was dimly aware of Sadie's ragged breaths, and that she'd smoothed her shirt back down, but she didn't move away. He hated to think what he must look like: grim; dark and forbidding; his scars a dark and vivid red. He must look an utter fright, a beast of a man. But she didn't move away.

'Enzo?'

Kiss her—you, with those scars?

It was the vision of his scars that hauled him back. What was he thinking? Sadie would see him as an object of pity, nothing more. He had scars enough to last a lifetime. He had no desire to acquire new ones—even if they were only to his vanity.

'Forgive me, Sadie. That walk was more taxing than I expected. Why don't you go for your swim while I rest for a bit, and then we can resume our conversation?'

Without waiting for her reply, he promptly lay back and placed his hat over his face—ostensibly to protect himself from the sun, but in actuality to ensure he didn't catch so much as a glimpse of Sadie's bare skin.

He counted to seven before he heard her move—clothes rustling and falling to the ground, soft footsteps in the sand moving away from him. The further away she moved, the easier it became to breathe. This attraction might be inconvenient, but he wasn't some hormone-riddled teenager. He was an adult and he *could* keep his reactions in check. Part of him hungered to join her for a swim—to be close to her effervescent sense of fun, to make her laugh if he could manage it, and just get out of his own head for a while—but…

Sadie hadn't flinched at the scars on his face, but the moment he removed his cargo pants he'd reveal the mangled mess of his leg. Not even Sadie would be able to pretend it was pretty. He didn't want to see horror and revulsion race across her face. He just…didn't have the heart for it.

Pushing the image from his mind, he forced himself to focus on his breathing. Eventually he found himself starting to notice the whispering of water against the shore and the melodic tweeting of the woodchats in the forest behind—easy, quiet, relaxing sounds. He frowned beneath his hat. This was…nice. Why hadn't he ventured outside sooner?

Lifting his hat a fraction, he dragged salt-scented air deep into his lungs. Hints of mimosa and jasmine seasoned the air—smells he associated with summer. The combined scents transported him back in time to a week he'd once spent with his mother, aunts and cousins at a modest seaside resort north of here when he'd been ten. The dramatic release in tension—of being away from his father and surrounded by kind, happy people who loved him—had been a revelation.

The sun warming his limbs, the scent of summer tickling his nostrils and the soft sound of Sadie splashing in the water—was that a light laugh he'd heard?—all had him letting out a long breath. The walk down had been arduous, but he *had* managed it. For the first time, he glimpsed a future in which he'd no longer be in pain, would no longer need his cane, and in which he'd feel hale and hearty once more.

Peace stole over him. He consciously relaxed his shoulders and jaw and concentrated on his breathing—a momentary surrender to the quiet, serenity, warmth and the scent of safety.

He came to, to find Sadie stretched out on her towel beside him—far enough away that he'd have to stretch out an arm to touch her—her eyes closed behind her sunglasses. She wore her T-shirt, but not her shorts. The T-shirt covered her to mid-thigh…

Don't look! He had no right to notice, let alone admire her curves.

'So…'

He started when she spoke, but another quick glance informed him her eyes remained closed, though a smile stretched across her lips.

'You're finally awake.' One eye opened and she peeked across at him. 'Do you know that you snore?'

'I do not!' He sat up. Did he? Nobody had mentioned it before. Reaching for his phone, he checked the time. *'Dio!'* He'd been asleep for two hours.

'Feel better?' She gave a lazy stretch, wriggling her back against her towel and clearly relishing the softness of the sand beneath. It filled his mind with forbidden images…

He slammed shut the vault of his mind. 'Much better.' He tested his leg—sore, but not too bad. 'I was grumpy after the walk down. I'm sorry.'

'I'm grumpy when I'm in pain too—the proverbial bear.'

She still lay back like a siren, her eyes half-closed, and he had to clench his jaw. He would *not* touch her.

'And I knew you weren't grumpy with me, Enzo, so it's okay. And you've given me all of this. How could I be anything but grateful?'

She sat up and his breath caught as her T-shirt lifted to reveal…more. She had long, shapely legs that made his heart pound and his mouth go dry. He'd bet they'd feel as silky as the water of the Mediterranean itself. 'I can't remember the last time I lay on the beach and…'

He dragged his gaze back to the view. 'Did nothing? Were lazy?'

'That's the one.'

'Did you enjoy it?'

'It was heaven.' She sent him a sidelong glance. 'Did you?'

He nodded. He felt like a new man, though he suspected the climb back up the hill would have him feeling like a grump again. Still; the fact he could feel this relaxed and this *well*—even if it was only momentary—was a revelation. Perhaps his family was right: perhaps he'd been brooding too much.

Admittedly, he'd had a lot to brood about, but so did the woman opposite. *Her mother has returned…* twenty-seven years after abandoning her. He made a vow to make sure Sadie had plenty of beach days over the course of the following fortnight.

Jumping to her feet, Sadie moved briefly out of sight before returning with a picnic basket. 'Luisa sent Guido down with our lunch, and with strict instructions that we're to leave the basket for someone to collect later. Apparently, if we do lug it back up the hill we'll be depriving someone of a swim. I suggest we do as we're told. It'd be bad form to deprive anyone of this.'

Sitting cross-legged on her towel, she opened the basket and examined its contents. 'Ooh, look at this.' She pulled out an antipasto board with cured meats, cheese and olives—enough to feed an army—along with a loaf of crusty sourdough bread and cans of icy-cold sparkling water. 'There are peaches and strawberries for after, and something else that looks wickedly sweet.'

He glanced inside. 'Sweet cannoli. I have a weakness for it.'

They attacked the food with gusto. Eventually Sadie gave a satisfied sigh and rested back, her hands propped behind her as she lifted her face to the sun. 'There's something about being somewhere beautiful in nature that's tonic for the soul. No wonder you retreated here for your recovery, Enzo.'

And, yet, if Sadie hadn't turned up he'd still have been locked inside the castle walls, brooding on all the ways he'd been wronged.

'You're lucky to have this place. What are your plans for it?'

'I expect I'll sell it.' Her instant shock made him wince. 'I know it's beautiful, but this place is tainted with memories of my father and grandfather. The *castello* has been the family's summer residence since the mid-1700s—but, as far as I can tell, all of my ancestors were ruthless, selfish men. I've no desire to align myself with them or to revere their traditions.'

He had no desire to turn it into his own pleasure palace, or develop it into an exclusive hotel for the rich and famous. Instead, he'd sell it to someone who would probably do that anyway, but which would be none of his business. He would donate the proceeds of the sale to his mother's charity, so that people who'd been abused and exploited would get the chance to break free from their abusers. His father and grandfather would turn in their graves if they knew—a thought that brought him pleasure.

But he didn't want to talk about any of that now. 'I'm glad you're enjoying your time here, Sadie. My father and grandfather wouldn't have approved of you—an honest, hard-working woman with no family wealth or connections—and that gives me a perverse pleasure.'

She clapped a hand over her mouth to stifle a bark of laughter, her eyes dancing. His lips twitched. 'But that is not what I wish to talk about.'

'You want me to answer the question you posed earlier.'

Reaching into the picnic basket, she pulled out a strawberry and lifted it to her lips. Enzo dragged his gaze away, his pulse revving like the engine of a sports car. He made himself shake his head. 'I know why you go above and beyond for Chelsea.'

Sadie pressed the back of her hand to her brow, like some swooning pantomime heroine. 'Because she was the one person who stood by me when everyone else had forsaken me.'

He knew she hammed it up to make him laugh, but it had the opposite effect. 'Why do you do that?'

'What?'

'Mock yourself like that?'

'I was just being silly…funny.'

'Well, it's not funny.' He glared. 'It's like some awful defence mechanism to put yourself down before anyone else gets the chance.'

She scowled and fidgeted. 'Shut up.'

'I promise to not make fun of you—not about stuff that matters.'

'No, you'll just shout at me,' she muttered, drawing agitated patterns in the sand, and it was his turn to shift uncomfortably. 'Fine,' she huffed. 'You promised not to shout any more, so I promise not to do that.' She grimaced. 'Or at least, I'll try. It's a kind of second-nature thing.'

A chasm cracked open in his chest and he rubbed a hand across it to try and ease the ache that settled there. He might find the grown-up version of Sadie challenging and somewhat exasperating, but she'd been the loveliest of girls as a teenager. She'd deserved better from the adults in her life. He knew the same loyal heart beat in her chest now as had then—even if that chest was now distractingly curvy and beautifully formed.

Not looking!

'Anyway, back to the conversation. You weren't really asking why I'd go to so much trouble for Chelsea. What you really want to know is why I came here; why I thought all of this was such a good idea. And there are a couple of different answers to that.'

She lifted her sunglasses onto the top of her head so she could meet his gaze, so he lifted his too. It seemed only fair. 'Okay.'

'First of all, remember the no-yelling thing.'

Damn. That didn't bode well.

'The thing is, you see, the thought of you here on your own, in pain physically and emotionally—' she gestured to his leg '—because of that cow Claudia…'

Things inside him clenched at the mention of his ex-girlfriend's name, even as part of him wanted to laugh at Sadie's word choice. But why did she think he'd been in love with her? That had to have come from Chelsea. He fought a frown. Did the rest of the family think Claudia had broken his heart too?

'Well, I hated the picture that formed in my mind.'

His attention snapped back and his eyes started to burn. She pitied him. His hands clenched. *Was that* why she was here—she *pitied* him? He reminded himself about not yelling.

'The thing is, Enzo, you were so kind to me when I was a teenager and had that huge crush on you. And I've never forgotten it.'

His hands unclenched. He flexed his fingers. 'You knew that I knew?'

'Only in hindsight.' She rolled her eyes. 'I was far from subtle.'

She'd been delightful, though.

'You could've crushed me utterly, but you didn't. You were thoughtful and lovely. You were careful not to raise my hopes, but never ignored me or treated me like a nuisance.' Her delightful nose wrinkled. 'I'm sorry if I was tiresome or a bother, by the way.'

'You weren't. You were lovely, Sadie. And if you'd been a little older…'

She laughed. 'As gallant as ever, but we both know I never had a chance with you, not really.'

The memory of that long ago kiss rose in his mind again. Sadie had been lovely, and he had been tempted, but his mother had read him the riot act in a way she'd never done before. Her domestic harmony had been so hard won; he hadn't wanted to do anything to shatter it. So he'd toed the line and had promised to stay away from his stepsister's best friend. He hadn't done anything that might rock the boat and endanger familial relationships.

And yet part of him had always wondered…

No, it didn't.

'I've always considered you a friend, Enzo, and I thought that, if I could come here and be a friend to you the way you were once a friend to me…' One shoulder lifted. 'Well, I wanted to do that if I could. Also—' her nose wrinkled again '—you never did like surprises and, when I couldn't talk Chelsea out of a *surprise* party, well, given everything that's happened this year, I thought you might like it even less now.'

His heart started to beat too hard.

'I thought maybe I could help smooth things over for everyone somehow.'

Somehow, without him realising it, she'd achieved her goal.

It struck him then how well she knew him. He also realised in that moment that he was going to agree to the party.

CHAPTER SIX

SADIE KEPT HER gaze trained on Enzo's face as she spoke and tried to track the expressions flitting through his eyes; tried to interpret what the shifting muscles around his mouth and eyes signified. She released a pent-up breath; anger, fury and outrage weren't emotions she could identify.

That didn't mean they weren't simmering beneath the surface, though. And he'd become dangerously serious when her remit was to try and cheer him up. 'Maybe me thinking I could come in and wave a magic wand was a dreadful cheek. What's that saying about the road to hell being paved with good intentions? Mind you—' she gestured at the view '—if this is hell…'

She winked, and one corner of his mouth hooked up into one of those devastating smiles that had never failed to make her knees weak as a teenager. It wasn't her knees that were the problem now, but the fire threading through her veins that had heat pooling in unmentionable places.

For all that's fair and holy, stop thinking of Enzo in that way.

'You are aware that you rabbit on with some dreadful nonsense?' he said.

Maybe so, but the tension in his shoulders had drained away, leaving him looking more relaxed. She'd take that as a win. 'But, in the interests of full disclosure, there's another reason I came to Italy.'

His gaze sharpened, and she lowered her sunglasses back into place. She started to reach for another strawberry, but changed her mind. Her stomach had knotted.

'I'm all ears.'

She hadn't meant to tell him any of this, but it felt oddly deceitful to withhold it. 'I wanted, maybe needed, to get away from home for a bit.'

'Damn it, Sadie, that sounds serious. Why?'

She opened her mouth to make some flippant remark, such as, 'Oh, the Trials and Tribulations of Sadie's Life: Part Three, in four-part harmony', or some such nonsense…

His frown deepened. 'Sadie?'

She flashed him a quick smile. 'Sorry, just remembering my promise about not mocking myself. Sometimes it feels good to make light of the hard stuff—a form of letting off steam.'

'Are you sure about that?'

No, damn it, she wasn't.

'If that's truly the case, then mock away.'

But she'd lost the urge. She stared down at her hands. 'The thing is, Enzo, after the best part of twenty-seven years my mother has decided to return home and declares she now wants to be part of her family's lives.'

'She's *returned*?'

He sounded suitably outraged… 'Chelsea told you, huh?'

He swore. 'Only that your mother had returned, nothing more.' He scrubbed a hand over his face. 'I imagine it is…'

'Confusing? Confronting? Infuriating?' she supplied when he didn't continue.

'All of those things, *sì*.'

The steady strength in his voice and its underlying warmth helped to ease some of the burning in her soul, but that burning only settled behind her eyes instead, and she found herself blurting out, 'It's awful, Enzo. Horrible.'

Unable to keep her agitation in check, she leapt to her feet. Seizing a pebble, she hurled it as hard as she could towards the water—falling well short. Stomping down, she picked it up and hurled it again. This time it made a satisfying splash.

She started at a soft touch on her arm. Enzo stood there, offering her another pebble. She took it and flung it so hard, her shoulder ached.

'Remind me at some point to teach you how to throw properly.'

The wry tone had a reluctant smile tugging at her lips.

'Tell me what's so horrible about it.'

'Besides the fact that she dumped me with her

parents and never contacted us once in twenty-seven years?' She thumped her hands onto her hips, finding it oddly disconcerting to be the object of such a concentrated gaze.

'Such behaviour is hard to forgive, *sì*.'

It was. And yet she'd been prepared to, except… 'I just don't like her.' Maybe it was due to their history—or *lack* of history. 'She hasn't offered any explanation for why she left all those years ago, and she certainly hasn't offered an apology. She's just waved it all off with, "I had things I wanted to do with my life", as if that makes it all right.'

She frowned at the far horizon. 'There's something hard about her. She's totally self-centred.' Her heart gave a sick kick. 'I think the real reason she's returned is she's run out of money, and now plans to live off my grandparents' generosity.'

'How have they taken this turn of events?'

She threw her hands in the air. 'They're beside themselves with joy.' For the first time in her life, she'd witnessed how they looked when they were truly joyful, and it had cut her to the marrow that she'd never managed to generate even the tiniest flicker of that in them in twenty-seven years. 'They've welcomed her with open arms. They've done the whole "fatted calf" thing. I know I sound bitter, but…'

She was so worried about them!

His gaze felt like a living thing on her skin,

making it prickle all over. 'What *aren't* you telling me?'

His perception took her off-guard and she had to swallow before she could speak. 'For one of the few times in my life, and probably the last, I kicked up a fuss and made a scene. I haven't done that since the rocking-horse incident. I've always done my best to be agreeable and undemanding; *pleasant*. Because despite my grandparents' lack of joy—' *former* lack of joy, she added silently '—they're good people and they never asked to be lumped with me.'

'Sadie…'

He halted when she lifted a hand. 'I'm not feeling sorry for myself, over-dramatising or mocking myself, Enzo. It's a statement of fact. Unpalatable, perhaps, but…'

He rubbed a hand over his face. 'I apologise for interrupting.'

She managed a smile. '*That* was a ten-out-of-ten apology.' Blowing out a breath, she stared out at the water. 'I told Verity—that's my mother—that her parents deserved an apology…and so did I. I said I understood a phone call might've been awkward, but how hard would it have been for her to send birthday cards or a Christmas card every year to let us know she was still alive? I told my grandparents Verity had been selfish and untrustworthy and that I was worried she'd take advantage of them *again*. I asked them to be careful and remain on their guard.'

'What happened?'

'Verity laughed in my face.' She rolled her eyes. 'Which I suppose I should've expected. I don't think she has any real scruples. My grandparents, though…' She kicked at the water, sending an arc through the air, the droplets sparkling in the sun. 'My grandparents told me that I'd either have to accept Verity into our lives or they'd have nothing to do with me.' They'd demanded she *apologise* to Verity.

'Dio!'

And then he said a very rude word that had her blinking. His anger made her feel both better and worse.

'They've loved her all her life. They've missed her and grieved for her for the last twenty-seven years. It makes no sense, but the heart wants what the heart wants.' And their hearts craved Verity.

'I'm sorry, Sadie.'

She was too.

'How have things been left?'

She ground her palms on her eyes. She pulled her hands away and clenched them at her sides. 'I've told them I want nothing to do with Verity. I told them that, if they ever need me, they only have to call. I told them I'll always be there for them. But that embracing Verity…' She shook her head. 'That's a step too far.'

Was she being selfish?

'What did they say to this?'

A lump lodged in her throat and it hurt to swallow. 'That I wouldn't be hearing from them.' She pounced on another pebble and hurled it. 'I feel like I've abandoned them, though. I've left them alone with a...*wolf*!'

A strong arm drew her in close to his side, and for a moment she let herself lean against him and let his strength filter into her.

'Your grandparents are neither naïve nor stupid.'

Except when it came to Verity.

'They're adults—old enough to make their own decisions and to live with the consequences. It's admirable that you wish to save them from pain, Sadie, but that's a choice they have to make for themselves. You can't make it for them.'

Enzo smelled like a forest—cool and woodsy, with a hint of something dark and green, like pine. She fought the urge to snuggle closer. He felt like rest, respite and safety.

'But I also understand it doesn't make it any easier.'

With his arm around her, she no longer felt so alone. She rubbed her cheek against the soft cotton of his T-shirt, relishing the feel of him beneath it. 'I was thinking of ringing them once a month—just to check in and see how they're doing. I mean, there's no guarantee they'll take my calls, but...' She squinted up at him. 'What do you think?'

'Keeping the lines of communication open and letting them know you're there for them if they need you?' His arm briefly tightened around her. 'It's a generous thing to do. It demonstrates how Verity should've behaved for all of these years.'

He thought she was generous…

Her gaze traced the line of his jaw across to surprisingly sensual lips and her mouth went dry. She imagined those lips lowering to hers… A pulse inside her kicked to life. She imagined Enzo kissing her—the two of them shaping their lips to one another's and deepening the kiss into something fierce and passionate. Rest, respite and safety fled. In their place burned need and hunger.

A gasp escaped her. His gaze swung down, raking over her face with a ruthless precision that tore through all her pretences. Those dark eyes rested on her mouth, darkening further. Hunger, fierce and intense, flared through them. His arm tightened. Her pulse went wild. He was going to kiss her…

The arm slipped from her shoulders and he took a step back.

Sadie blinked. *Oh, God. Oh, God. Oh, God.* She did what she could to rein in her raging pulse.

'*Sì*, Sadie, ringing your grandparents once a month is more than many people would do in your situation.'

She forced her mind to the conversation, pretending her body wasn't on fire for him. 'Thank you.'

He frowned at the water, his eyes narrowing

and his nose wrinkling. 'It makes me ashamed of myself.'

She jerked round, pouncing on the conversational lifeline he'd thrown to her. *'What?'*

'My family want to throw me a party and I'm acting as if it's the crime of the century. *Oh, woe is me.*' He pressed the back of his hand to his brow the way she had earlier, and she had a sudden insight into why he hated her self-deprecation. 'If Chelsea has her heart set on throwing me a surprise party…' He rolled those wonderfully broad shoulders. 'Rather than bellyaching about it, I ought to be grateful and submit with grace.'

A weight slammed down on her shoulders. 'And here we now are, on the road to hell.'

His brows lowered over his eyes. 'What do you mean? Why do you say this?'

'You, me and Chelsea—we're all in a bind of our own making, aren't we, due to our good intentions? Me wanting to help Chelsea and you; Chelsea wanting to help you and me; and now you're feeling guilty and feeling obliged to help me and Chelsea.'

That piratical brow lifted. 'And you think us all wanting to help each other is putting us on some figurative road to hell?'

'There are so many good intentions ricocheting about the place, they're like balls in a pinball machine! Or should that be gold paving stones?' She and Chelsea were forcing him to have a party he didn't want. That suddenly seemed terribly unfair.

'You're wrong about my sense of obligation, Sadie. I made the decision about the party while you were swimming—before you told me what had happened with your grandparents.'

She loved that he didn't mention Verity. That he'd dismissed her as the non-entity in Sadie's life she actually was. It was her grandparents' reaction that cut her so deeply, their hearts she feared for. But none of that made her believe him. He was being as gallant as ever, that was all. The weight on her shoulders grew heavier.

'You don't believe me.'

It was a statement, not a question. She glanced away from penetrating dark eyes and then started. 'Your stick is getting wet!'

'Does that matter?'

'It does if it's not waterproof.'

'I think you are once again trying to change the subject.'

So what if she was? The fact remained that they were wading in ankle-deep water and she wasn't sure how that had happened—had it been her agitation or his? But the salt water was probably doing nasty things to his cane—even if it happened to do lovely things to her over-heated flesh.

'While you were swimming, I forced myself to relax—consciously,' he said, ignoring her concern about his cane. 'You know the drill—unclench your jaw, relax your shoulders, breathe deeply.'

She found herself fascinated with the way his mouth formed the words. There was a decisiveness to the way he moved and spoke, but an innate sensuality to the shape of his lips. She knew from experience the devastating power those lips contained…

Once! He kissed you once!

And yet she'd never forgotten it. No kiss she'd had before or since had ever eclipsed it.

During that last summer she'd spent with Chelsea's family, Chelsea's father had announced he was throwing a ball in honour of Chelsea and Sadie finishing boarding school. Sadie could only stare at him when he'd told them. *She* was going to a real, live ball! It had been the most gobsmackingly glittering affair. Glamorous people had filled the ballroom, looking gorgeous; the champagne had flowed; waiters had circulated with the fanciest canapés she'd ever seen. There'd been a band and dancing. She remembered the lights, the laughter, the warmth…

Late in the evening, she'd retreated to the edge of the dance floor to stare at it all, determined to fix it in her mind forever.

'Enjoying yourself?'

That voice had immediately filled her stomach with a million fluttering butterflies. *Enzo.* 'It's amazing. I'm having a ball!'

They'd laughed at her accidental pun, but then his gaze had roved over her face and he'd shaken his head. 'Your hair…'

She and Chelsea had been fussed over by hairdressers and beauticians all afternoon. Her hairdresser had suggested a new cut, and on the spur of the moment she'd agreed. Her curtain of shoulder-length hair had been cut short, making her eyes look bigger and enhancing her cheekbones. She'd gazed at her reflection afterwards in wonder.

She'd touched it. 'Do you like it?' Her voice had grown confusingly breathy.

His eyes darkened. 'You look beautiful.'

The way he'd looked at her, she hadn't been able to utter a single word.

With a low laugh, he'd shaken himself. 'Why aren't you dancing? I've noticed you've not lacked for partners.'

Maybe it was the new haircut, all those glittering lights or the fact the night was nearly over, but she'd found herself saying, 'Why don't you ask me to dance?'

He held out his hand and she didn't hesitate. She'd always dreamed of dancing with Enzo, just once. The moment he pulled her into his arms, all the teasing lightness fell away, replaced with something far more exciting. 'I haven't been able to look away from you all evening.'

His words thrilled her. She lifted her chin, desperate to appear polished and poised, but their eyes locked and she couldn't look away, couldn't hide how much she wanted him. An answering hunger flared in his eyes and her heart stuttered. Enzo *wanted* her…

In a manoeuvre that thrilled her to the soles of her feet, he waltzed her behind a curtain to a private nook. He didn't release her, he just continued staring at her. She stared back. For the last five years, she'd dreamed about this man. Had he finally noticed *her*?

His eyes filled with an odd mix of fierceness and tenderness. 'I find myself aching to kiss you, Sadie.'

Her heart thundered so loud, she was sure he must hear it. 'I wish you would.'

His lips swooped down then and claimed hers in a devastating kiss that curled her toes. Wrapping an arm around her waist, he pulled her more firmly against him and she flung hers around his neck and kissed him back with inexperienced enthusiasm.

He stilled, and she worried she'd done something wrong, but then he kissed her again, slowly, teasing her tongue into a dance with his, teasing her to open herself up to him more fully. That exploration—the thoroughness of it and their delight in it—had a foreign heat gathering in her blood, a storm of sensation threatening to overwhelm her.

She needed more! And he gave her more until she was nothing but burning, writhing need, pressed so tightly against him that she could feel how much he wanted her too.

'Dio!'

Enzo lifted his head and she wanted to cry out a protest, but the sounds of the ballroom filtered back into her consciousness. They stared at one another, both breathing hard. 'This is not the time or the place for me to kiss you like this. Meet me in the garden tomorrow at ten.'

She nodded and, with a final kiss on her palm, he melted back into the crowd. Not a single moment in her life since had ever felt so full of possibility.

Sadie dragged her attention back to the present, her heart thundering. *Dear God.* What on earth was she doing, remembering that kiss? It had come to nothing then and it'd come to nothing now.

Shoving her shoulders back, she searched her mind for the thread of their conversation; what had they been talking about…?

'You relaxed…?' she said.

Enzo fought a frown. There was a funny edge to Sadie's voice that he couldn't account for. Was she worried about this party being forced upon him? He set himself to easing her mind.

'*Sì.* I started noticing the birds chattering away and the feeling of the sun on my skin.' Some of her curious tension eased. When she glanced up, he released a slow breath. 'There was a scent on the air that hurtled me back twenty years to a summer holiday I'd had with my mother's family. My father wasn't present and it was…joyous, peaceful. I remember feeling surrounded by people who loved me.'

Her face went soft. 'That sounds lovely.'

It had provided his mother and him with some

much-needed respite. 'We needed it. At the time my parents' marriage was particularly rocky and my father had a way of shouting—so savage and brutal. He'd loom over my mother and…'

She gripped his forearm, her eyes wide. 'Oh, Enzo, that must've been terrifying.'

He stared down at that small yet surprisingly strong hand, her touch unexpectedly comforting. When his gaze lifted, she blinked, and the gold flecks in her eyes seemed to pulse. For a moment it felt as if time itself had slowed. Bright eyes lowered to his lips and his heart surged against his ribs. Small teeth sank into the plump ripeness of her bottom lip and need seared though him.

Sadie pulled her hand back and a chill chased through him. What he felt for Sadie was madness. He would *not* indulge it.

'Was your father physically violent?'

She didn't look at him; she stared at the ground, at her feet, instead. He gritted his teeth and counted his breaths, trying to pretend his body wasn't on fire for her. 'He didn't get the opportunity. During one particularly torrid argument, I intervened—pushed him away from her and yelled at him to leave her alone. I was twelve.'

Wide eyes lifted and she asked, 'What happened?'

'My mother—realising what a detrimental affect their fighting was having on me and how toxic it all was—decided enough was enough. She left my father that afternoon.'

'Good for her!' Sadie's chin shot up, as if she was proud of his mother. 'And good for you.'

Warmth spread through his chest. It didn't dislodge the prickle of desire, but it helped temper it.

'Life became smoother then. The courts decreed that my parents share custody. But it was easier to deal with my father when my mother wasn't there.'

The glance she sent him said she didn't believe him.

He shrugged. 'So when I was lying on the beach and recalled that week with my mother's family…' She looked him square in the eye. He held her gaze. 'It reminded me that there can be strength and comfort in having the people you love around you.'

He clenched his hands, fighting the temptation to hook a hand behind her head, to swoop down and capture her lips with his. Her actions, if not her words, had made it clear she didn't want that to happen, even if he'd started to sense that she too fought an unwanted attraction to him. She'd have her reasons for wanting to keep her distance and he'd respect that.

Maybe it's the vile scars on your face.

He ignored the ugly taunt. That voice sounded too much like his father's, and he'd always made it a point of pride to take an opposite position to his father's opinions—prejudiced and biased as they were. The one thing his father hadn't been was progressive. Sadie wasn't like his father—she didn't care about his scars.

He wasn't like his father either. He would *not* attempt to seduce her. Nor would he try to convince her to indulge in a fling when she didn't think it in her best interests…his back molars ground together…regardless of how much he might want to.

Seducing Sadie should be the last thing on his mind. He needed to convince her they weren't on some imagined 'road to hell' of her making. He wanted to convince his family he was doing well. 'Remembering that long-ago summer holiday had me rethinking my desire to keep everyone at a distance. Seems a little stupid now, if you want the truth.'

That had her shaking her head. 'There's nothing *stupid* about you needing time to adjust.'

Perhaps not. Still, while the scars that Claudia had left him with would last a lifetime, his family shouldn't pay the price for that. 'I'm well on the road to recovery; I'm gaining strength every day. It's true I'm still self-conscious about my scars, and the fact I need to walk with a stick for the foreseeable future, but my family have already seen my scars. They saw me when I was in hospital and my leg was in traction. But my face is no longer swollen beyond recognition, my cuts and bruises have faded and at least I'm walking, even if it is with a cane—all of that will be an improvement to them.'

A frown continued to lurk in the hazel depths of her eyes. Planting his walking stick between them, he leaned on it with both hands. 'If Chelsea is worried enough to send you here, that means she's picked up from her father that he's worried, which means my mother must still be worried. If having a party will stop them all from worrying, then I will gladly have one.' He leaned closer, catching her eye. *'Gladly.'*

Her hands went to her hips. 'You're amazing, you know that?'

He straightened at her words. Odd, but for a moment he'd felt as if he could fly. He gestured to the path instead. 'You ready to tackle that again?' He might as well harness this strange energy while he could and use it to his advantage.

'Okay.' She clapped her hands. 'Let's do it.'

'What film are we watching tonight?' Enzo asked after another of Luisa's delicious dinners. For once, he'd cleaned his plate.

They moved through to the drawing room and he halted when he saw his father's collection of military memorabilia had been replaced with his grandmother's scent bottles. He stared at the new display, his jaw slack.

Beside him, Sadie fidgeted. 'You did say if I found the perfect spot… If you hate it, I'll move it first thing tomorrow. I just thought…'

'No.' The display of scent bottles somehow eased the hard, aggressive edges of the room, much like his grandmother's presence had when she'd been alive. 'It's perfect.'

Continuing through the drawing room to the sitting room beyond, he found himself frowning. It had taken on a new life with Sadie here—nothing glaring or obvious. She had a fondness for colourful cushions and cosy throw rugs. She'd made the sofa look like a little haven of holiday goodness. His chair now sported a fat cushion that looked oddly inviting, as if she hadn't been able to resist providing him with a spot of comfort and colour too. The thought made him smile.

'I'm afraid I've taken a few liberties, ordering some things online for this room. I hope you don't mind.'

He didn't know what it was about those amber flecks in her hazel eyes, but they could make him clench and melt at the same time. 'Not at all.'

'As for what film to watch tonight… I expected this to be a democratic household—uh, castle. I'm happy to take it in turns.' She stuck out a hip. 'If you're up to the challenge.'

He couldn't back down from that. He immediately sifted through his DVD collection. He could choose something modern—perhaps with an actress who also had beguiling eyes—or stay on theme with another older film, maybe even another Audrey Hepburn movie.

'*Roman Holiday.*' She'd love it even more than last night's film.

'Another I haven't seen!'

He might consider Audrey Hepburn beguiling, but his gaze repeatedly returned to Sadie during the film rather than remain on the screen. Her reactions to the lead characters' antics and dilemmas captivated him. Every time she laughed and happy-sighed, an unfamiliar warmth spread through his chest.

Internally, he rolled his eyes. Evidently he'd been hiding himself away from the rest of the world for a little too long. He'd never expected life to return to normal—not prior-to-the-accident normal—and he didn't now, but he'd started to sense that he could create a new normal.

Perhaps it was time to make a start: to return to Milan and work; to stare down the aggressively curious until he stopped being a novelty. Just as had Hepburn's character in the film, he'd had his time out. He could return to the world of work and duty, if not renewed then at least rested and ready.

The thought startled him. Sadie had been here for two and a half days and she'd already turned his world upside down. He wondered if she knew what an impact she'd had on him, just like Gregory Peck's character had on Audrey in the film.

When the film finished, Sadie turned to him. 'An excellent choice, Enzo. So fun.'

He fought a frown. He'd expected her to be more enthusiastic and gushing. 'But?'

She mocked-glared. 'They fell in love. They

were perfect for one another. They should've ended up together forever!'

Her words made him smile. 'You're still a romantic, then? But can't you see they came from different worlds? It would never have worked.'

She blinked and eased away a fraction, even though he sat in his arm chair and she'd curled up in a corner of the sofa.

'But meeting each other, spending time with each other, had a significant impact on their lives—made them better people. Don't you think that has a beauty and power of its own?'

'I suppose.' She clearly wasn't convinced.

'But?'

She stared at the now-blank TV screen, her eyes far away. 'But in two years' time they'll meet again after it's discovered he's the secret prince of a neighbouring kingdom.'

He couldn't help but laugh. 'Or it's discovered she's actually a commoner and is therefore free to marry whomever she pleases.'

'That could work too, but only if the new royal person is lovely.'

'And then *that* monarch could meet a commoner who changes his or her world for the better.'

'Or if the new monarch is a rotter…'

They bounced around increasingly ridiculous scenarios until they were both laughing.

'*Roman Holiday* was an excellent choice, Enzo.

I'm going to have to put my thinking cap on to try and top it.'

He looked forward to her next choice.

'I've also been thinking…'

He glanced back to find she'd uncurled her legs from beneath her, her feet now planted firmly on the floor and hands pressed together. Was she about to spring some new and unwelcome plan on him? Should he be worried? 'About…?'

'I don't like lying to Chelsea.'

It hit him then that Sadie didn't like lying full-stop.

She leaned towards him. 'The upside is, if Chelsea knows that you know about the party, then you get a say in the party prep.'

She was trying to get them off that good intention road to hell, and her generosity melted some of the hardness inside him. She'd be the one to take the heat in this particular scenario. Yesterday, he'd accused her of taking away his autonomy, but here she was, trying to give it back to him—and not just giving it back, but handing it to him on a gem-encrusted golden platter. She'd called him extraordinary earlier, but she was the extraordinary one.

He had no intention of causing a rift between Chelsea and her but he couldn't deny the pull of having a measure of control over the party. 'What if I told Chelsea I'd overheard you and Luisa discussing the party and confronted you with it? It's only a little white lie, but one that will save everyone's face.' And should cause zero trouble.

She bit her lip. 'That could work. And it's in the spirit of the endeavour.'

He couldn't explain why, but the fact they were now conspirators lifted his spirits. 'And will you help me throw a party that my family will never forget?'

Her entire face lit up, and that was worth whatever sacrifice he'd just made.

CHAPTER SEVEN

THE FOLLOWING DAYS took on a pattern. Sadie catalogued the toy collection for a couple of hours each morning and then she and Enzo headed down to the beach. The clifftop path was clearly a challenge, but Enzo simply gritted his teeth and got on with it.

She admired his determination. And the strength of the powerful muscles developing in his thighs. And the breadth of his strong, broad shoulders. And the piercing power of his eyes…

And. And. And. She found so much to admire in Enzo, it sometimes made her dizzy. It was *platonic* admiration, though. Maniacal laughter sounded in the back of her mind. Fine, okay, it was lustful ogling, but any hot-blooded woman would feel the same.

She'd learned not to make small talk when they reached the beach, but to leave him be to catch his breath. He might not be the snarling, snappy grump who'd greeted her on her arrival, but she didn't want to push her luck. Enzo had donned a gallantly good face about the party and she wanted to make the trial of that easier, not harder.

He didn't swim—perhaps the walk down and back was enough to test his leg—but she silently willed him to remember that long-ago holiday when he'd been a little boy and to…

What? an inner voice mocked. *Look forward to the party?*

She bit back a sigh. If only. What Enzo was no doubt looking forward to was the party being over. And her being gone.

If she thought she'd noticed heat in his eyes once or twice, it was best to ignore it. Nothing could happen between them. They were from two completely different worlds. She wasn't going to put at risk the future she was building for herself.

Shallow creature that she was, though, part of her exulted every time that brooding gaze darkened and lingered on her. It made her want to throw caution to the wind. But then his gaze snapped away and all the reasons why it would be a bad idea rushed back.

She couldn't forget what had happened nine years ago, the morning after the summer ball. Racing down to breakfast, she'd passed his mother's sitting room and had overheard Isabella mention her name.

'What are you doing, Enzo, with Sadie?' Her heart had stopped; so had her feet. 'This must stop! Sadie is not from our world. She doesn't have the resources to negotiate the world you come from.'

She hadn't stayed to listen to any more. She'd fled. She'd thought Isabella liked her. She'd thought the family considered her an equal, not the second-class citizen the girls at school had thought her. To discover that wasn't the case…

She'd buried her face in her hands. In her desire to be loved and to belong, had she misread the family's regard for her? Nausea had churned in her stomach and she'd had to take deep focussed breaths to fight a growing sense of panic. Would Enzo do as Isabella asked? she'd wondered. Would he…?

Her mind had frozen. She'd become nothing more than a bruising, aching throb. *Give him the benefit of the doubt.*

Enzo had met her in the garden as planned, and with her every atom she prayed he'd defy his mother's injunction. Instead of kissing her, though, he'd shaken his head and a dark chasm had opened up inside her.

'You're lovely, Sadie, but I fear the romance of the ball went to our heads. It feels deceitful to lead you on. For the next few years, I need to focus on my business, while you ought to be focussing on university.'

'I see.'

'My life is in Italy, while yours is here in Australia.'

They could work around a long-distance romance, Sadie thought. If he wanted to…

'I'm not looking to tie myself down,' he'd said.

So he didn't want to. She'd simply nodded and said, 'Very well.'

He'd turned and walked away and her heart had shattered into a million little pieces.

She'd cut short the rest of her stay—told them Pop was sick and Grandma needed her at home. She'd never told Chelsea about the kiss. That was the last summer she'd ever spent with Chelsea and her family. She'd been eighteen—an adult. It had been time to stop relying on the charity—the pity and kindness—of other people.

Don't let your guard slip now. She would *not* let Enzo break her heart a second time.

In the evenings, they watched films. She countered *Roman Holiday* with *Notting Hill*, which had made him laugh. His next choice had been *The Princess Bride* and hers had been *Crazy Rich Asians*. Afterwards, they curled up on their separate seats with books or laptops before retiring for the night.

In the afternoons, they went their separate ways. Sadie to restore some project that had caught her eye just for the fun of it, or to read the journals she'd found in the attics, which led her down rabbit holes of their own.

And Enzo to…who knew? Rest? Work? Have some alone time? She'd love to lure him outside the castle walls and end this self-imposed exile, but didn't know how to broach the subject. Part of her was reluctant to risk the harmony they'd forged. Maybe pushing him to have a party was enough. Still…just to explore the village on the opposite hill would be something.

A knock on the doorframe of the drawing room had her swinging around from the work space she'd set up on the table beneath the bay windows. She did her best to temper her surprise. 'Enzo!'

'Am I disturbing you?'

'Nope, I'm just tinkering. Come and see.' She held up a miniature wind-up robot. 'I've been trying to fix this, but the proof will be in the pudding. Let's see if I've been successful.'

Winding it up, she set it down and then clapped her hands as it lumbered down the length of the table, arms and legs moving in tandem. Enzo grinned. The grin remained in place when his gaze lifted back to hers.

Heart-thumping and vein-throbbing immediately commenced. Of all the things that were ridiculously attractive about Enzo—and that list grew longer every day—it was his smile that held the most power. When he smiled properly, he did it with all of himself, and it never failed to knock her off her axis.

'You fixed this?'

'The wind-up mechanism just needed some TLC. As do these ones here.' She gestured at the two tin figures partly disassembled in front of her. Glancing up at him, she pursed her lips. 'It's not hard. Would you like to give it a go?'

'I, uh…' He held up his hands. 'These are…'

Beautiful?

'Big and maybe clumsy. What if I break something?'

She cocked her head to one side. 'There's a quote I love, or maybe it's a social media meme; I can't remember. But it goes like this: "what if I fall?" And the response is, "Oh, my darling, but what if you fly?" Whenever I'm intimidated, I recite that and it gives me heart.'

She'd been using it *a lot* lately.

She gestured to the toys. 'There are no guarantees. The mechanisms are old. There's every chance they'll crumble the moment we touch them.' She leaned in closer and drew in his glorious woodsy scent. 'But I'll let you in on a little secret—if that does happen, I can order replacement parts. I believe I have several in my work bag already.'

That made him smile again. *Don't stare.* 'Or, we could strike gold like we did with this robot here and they'll magically come to life again. The only way to know is to give it a shot.'

'I'm game if you are.'

'Pass my laptop over and I'll get it out of the way.'

He did as she bid, but the movement woke her computer from its sleep mode. She'd forgotten to close the app she'd been working in and a document she'd been going over earlier sprang to life.

Notice of Resignation: Sadie Beckett.

Swallowing a squeak, she leapt forward to snap the lid closed and move the laptop to the coffee table where it could safely hide all her secrets. Her heart pounded. Had he seen the document? Would he ask what the hell she was doing with her life?

But, when she turned back, she found him studying the disassembled toys, his brow pleating as he tried to work out how they all fitted back together. Letting out a slow breath, she returned to the table and set him up with the necessary tools then walked him through what to do.

Eventually they put the toys back together. Holding their breath, they wound them up and set them on the table. A ballerina on a pedestal twirled for all she was worth, while a flamingo flapped its wings and bobbed its neck.

Swinging to each other, they high-fived, grinning madly.

'You need to visit the artisan centre.'

She blinked. 'The what?'

'Some artisans in the local village have formed a cooperative—an artisan centre—in a renovated stable yard. You ought to visit before you go home.'

Her heart thumped. 'Would you take me?' She

clasped her hands beneath her chin and prayed he'd say yes.

His face shuttered and her heart nose-dived.

The resistance rose through Enzo immediately.

Why? Was he really that reluctant to show his face in public?

Yes.

But he couldn't shake off the sight of the resignation letter he'd seen when he'd moved Sadie's laptop, and the way she'd snatched her computer from him… His every instinct had warned him not to say anything.

Why had she resigned? Was she unhappy in her current position? Was it because of her mother, or her grandparents?

Chelsea hadn't mentioned any of this. Did she know, or was Sadie keeping it from Chelsea because she was pregnant and didn't want to worry her? His hands clenched.

'Never mind. It was a silly suggestion.'

He hated the way Sadie's face deflated. She was making huge changes in her life and who did she have to offer her support? The people who should be supporting her had turned their backs. He silently called them every bad name he could think of.

She pasted on a big smile. 'What kind of artisans are there?'

'No toymakers, but there's a jeweller and a violin-maker.'

'A violin-maker!' She made it sound like the most amazing thing in the world.

Half an idea formed.

What if I fall?

Oh, but my darling, what if you fly?

'There's a shoemaker and a potter. And a candlemaker too, I think.' It had been a long time since he'd visited the village. He stared at the toys they'd just mended. She was doing all this work when she didn't have to. He thrust out his jaw. 'Yes. I'd be honoured to take you to see the artisans, Sadie.'

He wasn't sure who was more surprised by the offer—Sadie or him. She swung round from where she'd started to pack away her tools. 'Yes?' she checked, as if to make sure she'd heard him correctly.

'*Sì*, I will take you into the village.' Or, at least, he'd have Guido drive them. His leg needed more rehab before he could drive. She continued to stare at him as if he'd shocked her speechless. Rather than making him self-conscious, he found himself fighting a laugh. 'It is a KPI you can tick off in your report for my family—get Enzo outside the castle walls for an afternoon. You can write something like, "while not exactly garrulous, Enzo was polite and played well with others".'

Myriad expressions flitted across her face. 'Was that…*a joke*?'

'Sì.'

A slow smile spread across her face, to become an enormous grin, and then she started to laugh. She laughed so hard she had to hold onto her makeshift work bench to remain upright.

Something inside Enzo shifted. To see Sadie so utterly delighted electrified him. He wanted to do it again and again. 'Come, we'll go now.'

'Wait, what…*now*?'

'Do you wish to give me time to change my mind?'

'No.' She bit her lip. 'But do I have time to change? These are my work clothes and I look a fright.'

She looked delectable, but he couldn't say that. A funny ache took up residence in his chest. She was supposed to be on holiday, and clearly viewed this little jaunt into the village as a treat. If she wanted to fuss a little… 'Of course.'

'I only need ten minutes.'

'Take half an hour.' That would give him a chance to make the arrangements with Guido, and perhaps he would change his clothes too.

'Oh, Enzo, thank you!'

She hugged him, a quick, exuberant squeeze that was over before he had a chance to respond. He watched her dash from the room in the direction of the stairs, his heart thumping against the walls of his chest. It was such a small thing, taking her into the village, and yet it brought her so much happiness. He couldn't find it in himself to regret it, even if people did look at his scars and recoil. Or, worse, respond with pity. He ground his teeth together. He *could* do this.

The drive into the village took only fifteen minutes. Sadie leaned forward in her seat to take in as much as she could. On the spur of the moment, Enzo directed Guido to drop them at the piazza rather than the artisan centre. He would indulge her curiosity and delight. She'd earned it.

She stared around the square, with its quaint fountain and tubs of flowers. She stared as they negotiated tiny alleyways and took steps that led further up the side of the hill, opposite to the one on which Enzo's castle was perched. She stared at the landscape that opened up around them.

While Enzo did his best not to stare at her. She wore a red sundress dotted with white daisies and a pretty pair of sandals, and she looked the picture of summer. He was glad he'd taken the trouble to change into a pair of tailored navy trousers and a casual button-down shirt in a striking shade of earthy brown. The way her eyes had briefly flared when she'd seen him in them had made things inside him purr with satisfaction. *Not* that he was focussing on that.

'The village is amazing,' she breathed.

Was it? He tried to see it through her eyes: the cobbled streets that lent the village a mediaeval atmosphere; the warm, golden hue of the stone houses; the avenues of olive and cherry trees; the pots of rosemary and sage that scented the air;

the cheerful chatter that drifted from the tavernas and restaurants as they ambled past.

Actually, it *was* charming.

'Don't frown.'

He shook himself. 'I forgot how much I liked this place. I used to escape down here whenever my father became too much.'

'Did you have a favourite haunt?'

'Several.' There was a taverna where he'd always been welcome to join the other patrons in a game of cards or dominoes, and a tiny restaurant that had served wholesome homely meals which had somehow provided him with more than physical nourishment.

He waited for her to demand to hear more—to ask him to take her to these places—but she didn't. His eyes narrowed. Why not? Was she using some dastardly form of reverse psychology?

Enough with the suspicions!

Sadie wasn't being manipulative. She was probably doing all she could to be on what she saw as her best behaviour. She was probably thinking she'd already demanded too much of him today.

Damn it! Why couldn't her grandparents see what a gift Sadie was?

The moment they reached the stable yard with the artisans in their individual workshops, Sadie went into transports of delight. She bought a beautifully tooled leather diary from the leather-maker, a new straw hat from the hat-maker, earrings, candles and a new pair of shoes. She bought tote bags from the bag-maker to carry them all in.

Eventually, he said, 'Sadie, you do *not* need a violin.'

'No, but…maybe I need a new hobby.'

'How do you propose we carry all of this back down the hill?'

'Oh.' Her face fell.

'We can come back another day. You don't have to buy everything now.'

Which immediately cheered her up. 'It's such a treat to see all of this, Enzo. Thank you.'

He wrestled with himself for two-tenths of a second. In truth, though, he'd probably lost this particular fight days ago. 'Would you like to stay on in the village for an early dinner? There's a little place I know…'

Her entire face lit up. 'Yes, please!'

They ate in the tiny courtyard of his favourite restaurant that had a view of the countryside. The proprietor greeted him like an old friend. As others had done today, the man surveyed his face and nodded. There was no pity in his eyes, not even sympathy. It was just an acknowledgement, and Enzo found that was something he *could* bear.

Sadie took a sip of the local Vermentino he'd ordered and her eyes fluttered in appreciation. 'Delicious!' Mischief flashed across her face. She touched her glass to his. 'To ticking off KPIs.'

He tried not to grin too widely at her teasing.

'You're really well liked by the locals, Enzo.'

Her words made him blink.

'It must be nice to be back.'

'I…' He hadn't realised how much he would enjoy it. 'Yes.' He sipped his wine. 'You know, Sadie, I could see you in a little place like the artisan centre, working on your dolls and toys.'

It was her turn to blink. But then she pasted on a big, fake smile. 'You know what? I can too. But not quite yet—the time isn't right.'

Why not? She'd just resigned! Surely there couldn't be a better time?

'So.' She propped her chin on her hand. 'Have you had any thoughts about the kind of party you want?'

He bit back a groan.

'Because I've had oodles.' She bounced in her seat. 'Make me your party planner!'

'You *want* to be my party planner?'

'I've never planned a party in my life! It must be the best fun.'

A giant throb settled at the centre of him. *Damn it.* 'Fine! You can be my party planner.'

She gave an excited wiggle. 'Okay, how many people were you thinking of inviting?'

'Hmm… Mum and Stephen, Chelsea and Dominic…and you and me.'

She folded her arms and waited. When he didn't add any additional guests, she shook her head. 'That's not a party, Enzo. It's a dinner reservation.'

A scowl lowered through him.

'Remind me why we're having this party,' she ordered.

'To make my family happy. To stop them from worrying about me,' he said grouchily.

'Do you really think a dinner party of six is going to convince them you're well on the road to recovery—physically, emotionally and vocationally?'

He rolled his shoulders. 'Fine! How many extras were you thinking of?'

Behind the hazel of her eyes, he could see her mind racing. 'What about the cousins, aunts and uncles who were on that long-ago summer holiday?'

He sat up a little straighter. *Okay, that could work.* 'It would be like a mini family reunion.' His mother would love that. 'Very well.'

'And what about your besties? They'd be hurt to be left out.'

'You're like a dog with a bone. How about we just focus on eating our food?'

Which, luckily, chose that moment to arrive.

'You can give it some thought and get back to me. You don't need to decide today.' Sadie picked up her cutlery and gave one of those happy shimmies. 'This looks delicious! Thank you for today, Enzo. It's been wonderful.'

She sent him such a smile that he almost found himself almost agreeing with her.

CHAPTER EIGHT

ENZO FOLLOWED SADIE into the pool house the following afternoon. 'You think I should have a pool party?'

'Absolutely! But we don't want it looking like this.' Her hands went to her hips. 'It's awful! It's like a Las Vegas show hall.'

Her nose wrinkled, as if she'd stepped in something nasty, and a laugh pressed against the back of Enzo's throat. Guests didn't enter this pool house and wrinkle their noses. They pushed their shoulders back, assumed bored expressions and hoped some obsequious tabloid photographer was lurking in the shadows and that they'd find themselves in the society pages of some sophisticated magazine in the near future.

Memories of parties he'd been forced to endure here as a teenager flitted through him—his father and grandfather had held court like entitled pashas. The male guests had sized up Enzo and told him he had a lot to live up to. The women had flirted and sometimes touched him, making it clear they'd love to bed the Lombardi heir.

He'd learned early how to extricate himself from the clutches of the predatory and the insatiable, the social climbers and the scandal mongers. Perhaps that was why he'd always found Sadie's schoolgirl crush on him such a panacea—it had asked nothing of him, had expected nothing, and she'd been so darn sweet. Part of him—a secret, hidden part—had half-wished she'd been three or four years older. Maybe then…

Don't be daft. Schoolgirl crushes by their very definition were immature—built on daydreams and fairy tales, all rainbows and unicorns. They weren't designed to withstand the harsh realities of a messy world.

Yet knowing Sadie, spending summers with her as a part of his mother's new circle, had prevented him from becoming too jaded. He'd loathed his father's world, but had come to see it as just one tiny corner of the world. The world his mother had carved out for herself had been an altogether different one. There, he'd been able to find peace, acceptance and an innocence that had soothed his soul.

He recalled his mother's reaction when he'd kissed Sadie that one time, and winced. She'd called him into her sitting room the following morning…

'Sadie is an innocent. This has to stop! She's not from our world. She doesn't have the resources to negotiate the world you come from. Four years may not seem like much of an age dif-

ference to you, but there's a world of difference between eighteen and twenty-two. Think of all you've experienced in the last four years.'

He'd wanted to argue, but couldn't. He'd spent the previous four years at university—a time that had defined him and had helped him choose the future he'd wanted. And yet he'd found a connection with Sadie that previous night that he'd ached to explore further.

'This has to stop! Your father and grandfather would eat her alive.'

Her words had chilled his blood. Sweet and vulnerable Sadie would have no armour against their sophisticated barbs and mockery, their malice. And he'd known he wouldn't always be there to protect her.

'And if you're only toying with that lovely girl—delighting in her hero-worship of you to boost your own ego—then that would make you no better than your father.'

Nausea had churned in his stomach. Was that what he was doing?

'Young men can be reckless and thoughtless, but I raised you better than that.'

He'd sworn to never follow in his father's footsteps.

'She is your stepsister's best friend and is as dear to her as either you or I. If you were to cause Sadie pain, it could cause a rift between you and Chelsea that we might never be able to mend. And, Enzo, is a brief flirtation worth that?'

He'd wanted to argue that maybe it wouldn't be brief, but Sadie had been only eighteen. She'd had her whole life in front of her. What right had he had to influence her life at that time? *None.*

He'd shaken his head. *'No.'*

He'd never been able to forget that kiss, though. It had been full of hope and wonder. It sure as hell hadn't felt wrong. But beneath the surface innocence a shocking and bright carnality had lifted its head and roared to life, shocking him with its intensity. It was all he'd been able to do at the time to step away before he'd lost his head.

'Enzo.'

He snapped to, something in Sadie's voice informing him it wasn't the first time she'd called his name. 'Sorry?'

'You were miles away.'

He tried to get the raging of his pulse under control. 'Merely remembering the parties I was forced to endure here. Why, I wonder, did I toe the line rather than refusing to attend?'

'It was probably easier to grit your teeth and submit for a couple of hours than get into a fight with your father.'

Where possible, Enzo had avoided drama, temper tantrums and ugly displays of emotion—especially when it had come to his father. It had been oddly satisfying to keep an unemotional distance between himself and the older man. It had infuriated his father. As Enzo hadn't openly defied him, though, there had been little he could do about it.

As soon as Enzo had come of age, and after his grandmother had died, he'd cut all ties with his father, making it clear how much he loathed him and his lifestyle. He'd expected—*hoped*—to be disinherited. There'd been no money left—only debts and the castle. He wondered if that had been his father's revenge—forcing on him this place that held only bitter memories.

It *had* provided him with a retreat when he needed one, though.

He shook himself. 'Come, Sadie, let's chase those less than salubrious memories away. Describe to me your vision for this party.'

'You're making my day, Enzo.'

She feigned swooning, and her silliness chased his moroseness away.

'First of all, we need to move all of this ridiculous furniture out of here. You must have a shed somewhere we can store it.'

'We'll throw it.'

She stared down her nose at him. 'That's a waste. Sell it.'

'So I can stumble across it at some party I attend in the future? No, thank you.'

'Then donate it to an orphanage or a women's shelter or a nursing home where you won't stumble across it. Where people will use it and enjoy it.'

He grinned. 'That is a brilliantly devious plan.' His father would turn in his grave.

He raised his hand and she high-fived him without hesitation. Was it his imagination or did her breath hitch as their palms made contact? Their gazes caught and a primal surge of heat gathered in his veins. If he kissed her now, would she kiss him back the way she had when she'd been eighteen?

Sadie snapped away before that vision could fully form in his mind. Her chest rose and fell, and his heart thundered in his ears. She wanted him; he was sure of it. He did his best to keep his voice even. 'So we get rid of all the furniture. What then?'

'We go retro.'

He had visions of tall potted palms and elegant colonial-style furniture. It would be an improvement.

Sadie made a frame with her hands, as if she were a photographer. 'I'm thinking geometrical patterns and primary colours; futuristic furniture and lava lamps; inflatable bubble sofas and silly pool toys…'

His jaw dropped. '*1960s* retro?'

She danced on the spot and silently screamed. 'Oh, go on, Enzo, say yes. I know it's silly and probably dreadfully unsophisticated, but think how much fun it would be.'

Was this the kind of party she'd wished for

growing up? An ache started up in the centre of his chest.

'Can you imagine the looks on everyone's faces when they see it? They'll be beside themselves. There'll be fun, boppy sixties surf music belting from the jukebox—'

'A jukebox?'

'There *has* to be a jukebox.'

The crazy thing was, he *could* see it. His mother would clap a hand over her mouth to temper her laughter; Chelsea would probably spin on the spot until she was dizzy. Everyone would have a ball. In fact, they'd be too busy having fun to quiz him too closely. Nothing would symbolise his recovery more than the party Sadie described.

'We must have a huge bowl of fruit punch,' he said.

'And serve pizza.'

Resting his cane against a table, he moved more fully into the pool house and turned three-hundred-and-sixty degrees, imagining what it could look like.

'Believe me, Enzo, nobody can be sad when "Yummy Yummy Yummy" by Ohio Express is belting out of the jukebox.' She stuck her nose in the air at his raised eyebrow. 'I know what I'm talking about. I found a bunch of vinyl records in an attic once. Utter gold.'

'How much did they fetch?'

Sadie moved beside him to stare into the water of the pool, the surface reflecting the light back to make patterns on the walls. 'Oh, they weren't worth anything. The owner wanted to pay me to get rid of them. I convinced her to take fifty dollars for them. They were worth every penny.'

She'd bought them? He couldn't help but laugh.

She clapped her hands. 'That's beside the point. What do you think—shall we do it? Shall we throw a 1960s pool party?'

'Sì.' He recalled the resignation letter on her laptop and was careful to keep his shrug casual. 'Perhaps it's time for a career change. You could become a party planner.'

'I doubt it'd be as much fun if I was being paid for it.'

The sparkle in her eye, and the flush in her cheeks—her sense of fun—was somehow infectious. She was doing this for Chelsea and his family. For him. Obligation didn't weigh her down, though. She embraced the task with joy, despite all the other stuff happening in her life.

The last of his resistance to the party drained away in the face of her generosity. Reaching out, he squeezed her shoulder. 'Thank you.'

'Thank *you* for indulging my party planning fantasies.' She turned in his hold. 'I…' Her words petered to a halt at whatever she saw in his face.

'I'm even starting to believe I too will be transformed by…' He gestured to the room and frowned. 'What was the name of your song—"Yummy Yummy Yummy"?'

She nodded, but he suspected she was only half-listening as her gaze roved over his face.

His pulse picked up speed. 'You have breezed into my *castello* and now I can't remember why I was so cranky. You want to sprinkle a bit of fairy dust around and…'

'And?'

'I find myself at a loss to tell you how truly grateful I am.'

He didn't just see the way his words melted her, he felt it beneath his hand as her shoulder softened. His fingers, tender but hungry, curved around that shoulder and he ached to explore all of her—to run his hands down the length of her spine to her hips, to pull her in close and mould her to him. To feel her tense up again with an entirely different sensation.

Gritting his teeth, he ordered himself to behave, but for the life of him he couldn't let her go; he couldn't make his fingers uncurl from around her shoulder. 'Sadie, thank you.'

She pressed trembling fingers to his lips. 'No, don't. I'm so happy to be here, Enzo. I…'

He kissed her fingers. He didn't mean to. But his free hand lifted to hold her fingers against his lips and he pressed a kiss there—pressed a kiss to those sweet, elegant, *generous* fingers.

She gasped, as if his lips charged her with electricity, which was exactly how it felt—a charge racing from her fingers to his lips and then to his groin, the entire surface of his skin tingling and heating.

When she didn't move away, he did it again, his tongue darting out to taste her. Her scent rose up all around him—fresh, floral and more potent than alcohol. Her lips parted and her breathing grew ragged, but it was the hunger in her eyes that sent exhilaration racing through him. He doubted she was aware of it, but the fingers of her free hand gripped his forearm as if to help her remain upright.

'Enzo…'

His name emerged husky with need and he slipped an arm around her waist and drew her close, the press of her breasts against his chest the sweetest torture. 'You are beautiful, Sadie. And I'm tired of pretending I don't want you when my every atom craves you.'

She swallowed and nodded. She stared at his mouth as if hungry for his kiss, and he was more than happy to sate that hunger. Slowly dipping his head towards hers, her mouth lifted towards his as if in anticipation. He paused to relish the moment…

She blinked. 'But…'

He froze.

'Oh, God. We can't!' Sadie pushed away, panic streaking through her eyes. He let her go immediately but he'd forgotten exactly where they were, where they were standing. She took another step back.

'Sadie!'

He reached for her, but it was too late. Comprehension dawned over that beautiful face as she windmilled wildly before falling backward into the pool.

CHAPTER NINE

THE COLD DASH of water should've shocked Sadie to her senses, but the water wasn't cold enough for that. She wished it was January and the water frigid. She wished this water had the ability to dispel the hard, insistent ache beneath her breast bone…and other parts of her body.

But, as she gazed up at Enzo and blinked water from her eyes, all she could think was pulling him into the water too and having her wicked way with him. Thank God he wasn't wearing a business tie that she could reach up, wrap around her hand and…

Frustration ground from her throat and she flounced—had she ever flounced before in her whole entire life?—to the wide, shallow steps and stomped back onto dry land.

Enzo handed her the thickest of fluffy towels and for some reason that only fed her temper. If he laughed…

What?

She buried her face in the towel. If they laughed it might dispel some of the tension that had her wrapped up tight; might turn that near-kiss into something silly and trivial rather than something freighted with the weight of the world.

'Sadie…'

She lifted her head.

'Would it help if I threw myself into the pool as well?'

She let out a careful breath. Maybe they could pretend that moment had never happened. 'I'm tempted to say yes, but…'

Being soaked to the skin would plaster his T-shirt and chinos to his body like a second skin, and his body was already distracting enough. With a shake of her head, she set about drying her hair.

'We need to talk about what just happened.'

Damn it! 'Okay, fine.' Okay and fine *were not* what this was. 'But not here in Liberace's palace. This place is like the set of some terrible 1980s TV series like…like *Dynasty*.' Angsty drama wasn't the vibe she was aiming for.

'If you want to get out of your wet things first…'

Sadie led the way outside and flung herself down at a table on the terrace, angling her face to the sun. Closing her eyes, she gestured vaguely in the sky's general direction. 'I'll dry off soon enough.'

He hesitated and then sat too. 'Very well. First of all, if I misinterpreted your wishes and reactions just then, Sadie, I humbly apologise. I—'

'We both know you didn't misinterpret them.'

More's the pity. She'd wanted him to kiss her. But she'd pulled back for a reason—a reason that hadn't gone away. She slanted a glance in his direction. 'That was a ten out of ten, by the way.'

Her words didn't lighten the moment. He didn't smile.

'Then may I ask why you pulled back? You looked *horrified*.'

She sat up a little straighter. 'You don't think I did it because of your scars, do you?'

He shrugged, but she recognised the turmoil burning in the dark depths of his eyes, and bit back a sigh. 'It wasn't because of your scars, Enzo.'

Her gaze travelled to the thick red scar bisecting his forehead. 'This is probably a dreadful thing to say, but I like your scar.' It took all her strength not to reach out and trace it with her fingertip.

'You *like* it?'

'It's official, right? I'm going to hell.' He continued to stare and she did her best not to fidget. 'I honestly and truly wish you hadn't had to go through the pain you did to acquire that scar. But…it hooks up your eyebrow in this particular way.'

She tried to demonstrate, trying to mould her eyebrow into the same shape with her fingers. 'I can't decide whether that look is teasing or sneering, but either way it's totally…' To say 'compelling' would give too much away. 'Intriguing,' she settled on instead.

He continued to stare and she shifted on her seat to glare out at the water. That view ought to be soothing—all sparkling sea and soft sky framed by cliffs and verdant forests—but she doubted anything could currently soothe her. 'Given time, your scar will thin and fade and become even more artistic.'

'Artistic?'

'Yes! And it's probably wrong on so many levels, but it's how I feel, and you wanted the truth. I didn't pull back from kissing you because of your scars, Enzo; I can assure you of that. I pulled back because…'

Her glare became a scowl and she kept it trained on the view rather than turn it on him, no matter how much she might want to. He couldn't help feeling the way he did any more than she could, or any more that her grandparents could about Verity. He leaned across the table, as if hanging on her every word, and it was horribly heady.

Don't let it go to your head.

'I pulled back because Claudia broke your heart and I am *not* going to be your rebound fling.' She deserved better than that. And, for the first time in her life, she'd started to see that maybe she deserved better in other areas of her life too.

He swore. 'I knew that would come back to bite me on the butt.'

It was her turn to blink. She tried to raise an eyebrow—unsuccessfully—so pushed it up with a finger. Finally, he smiled, and her heart pitter-pattered. 'You want to explain what you mean?'

'I mean Claudia *didn't* break my heart. I should've corrected you when you assumed it on that first day, but I was too busy being grumpy.'

'But…you went so pale when I mentioned her name. Then when I told you how I got over my crush on you—in the hope it might help you get over Claudia—you scoffed and said it wasn't the same thing.'

He sent her an incredulous stare. 'You were referring to Claudia? I thought you were referring to me not being able to walk properly, and my scars, getting over the accident and how much my life had changed.'

Her jaw dropped.

'And I did not *scoff.* You've completely misread the situation.' He frowned. 'You've had this from Chelsea, right? She thinks Claudia broke my heart?'

Sadie didn't say anything, just shrugged.

'Well, you can tell her my heart isn't broken and that I'm actually glad to be rid of the woman.'

A weight lifted, like magic, easing the tension in her shoulders, her chest and her jaw. Settling back, she tried to fight a smile. He hadn't been in love with Claudia… She wanted to high-five someone.

The view acquired a new sparkle—all that summer magic shimmered with promise.

'What nobody knows is that I'd broken off with Claudia the previous week. It had been amicable enough, or so I'd thought. When she asked if I'd still escort her to a charity ball her grandmother had organised, I agreed.'

Because he wouldn't want to leave her high and dry, Sadie thought. Because he was a good guy. His other words filtered into her consciousness and things inside her started to tighten again. The accident had occurred on the way home from that charity ball.

'You said you *thought* it was amicable…which implies you were mistaken?'

'Wildly mistaken.' His lips twisted. 'A fact I discovered when I drove her home that evening.'

She went cold all over. 'What happened?'

He dragged a hand down his face. 'Damn it, Sadie, I wasn't going to mention any of this.'

'Too late.' The shadows in his eyes made her chest ache. 'You're going to have to tell me what *this* is now.'

Blowing out a breath, he tapped a finger against the table before straightening. 'During the drive home she wanted us to get back together, and outlined all the reasons we were good together.'

Sadie sucked her bottom lip. 'But you didn't agree.'

'What I'd forgotten to take into account was the fact that Claudia has rarely heard the word "no". Her father is a transport magnate and her parents have indulged her every whim.'

'But you couldn't be bought or brought to heel.'

'Correct.'

She stared at his scar and acid burned a path through her insides. 'She caused the accident.' Her heart pounded with big, hard, bruising thumps. 'She caused the accident,' she repeated, thinking she might be sick.

Dark eyes met hers. 'Inadvertently, yes.'

Her lungs started to burn.

'She lashed out at me—physically.'

'She *hit* you?'

'We were on a particularly dangerous piece of road and it took me completely off-guard. She had this hard little clutch bag and walloped me right here with it.' He pointed to his temple. 'And then tried to undo her seatbelt, presumably to get into a better position to keep hitting me. I had my hand over hers so she couldn't release the catch, so I was driving with one hand when she hit me again with that damn clutch. I lost control of the car, though thankfully I'd managed to slow down, so we didn't hit the tree at full speed.'

Her heart pounded in her throat. 'You could've gone over the cliff! She could've killed you both.'

He turned grey. '*Sì.* It has taken all of these months for that vision to stop waking me in the middle of the night.'

The darkness in his eyes had a lump lodging in her throat. Reaching across, she slipped her hand inside his. 'I'm sorry, Enzo. That was a truly terrible thing to go through.' She squeezed the life out of his hand, but he didn't seem to mind.

'I know it's an ugly story, but…'

'Why haven't you told anyone?' Why hadn't he made it public?

She found her hand suddenly empty and she nursed it in her lap, trying to rub away the feel of him. She needed to find a way to control the inconvenient feelings that gripped her whenever Enzo was near. There might not always be a convenient swimming pool to hurl herself into.

Enzo might not be nursing a broking heart, but he was in no shape for any kind of romantic entanglement. He needed rest, respite and a friend. Not the drama of a temporary love affair.

Would it be temporary?

Of course it would! As Isabella had pointed out nine years ago, Sadie would never fit into Enzo's world. The only thing that had changed was their ages, not their circumstances. He'd agreed with his mother then and he would again now.

When she'd left Australia, Sadie had told herself she was through with not measuring up, with not being *enough.* She wasn't going to let Enzo make her feel less again now. He mightn't mean to, but she was building a new life—a good life—and she wasn't going to put that in jeopardy.

Nor would Enzo want her to. The best the two of them could manage was something along the same lines as *Roman Holiday*. Her mind started to race.

That has merit.

Stop!

'Claudia did not emerge unscathed from the accident, Sadie.'

She dragged her attention back to the conversation. Claudia had broken her arm and fractured her collarbone. She'd suffered numerous cuts and abrasions—though not as seriously as Enzo.

'She suffered too. It seemed mean-spirited to point a finger in her direction—unnecessarily dramatic. She knows she caused the accident and will have to live with that knowledge for the rest of her life. That is punishment enough.'

He was too gallant. 'You should tell your family.'

He swung back, a frown on his face.

'They'll respect your desire for secrecy, but they love you, Enzo, and deserve to know what really happened.'

'You think that they will see it as an indication that I'm getting better.'

He *was* getting better, even if he couldn't see it for himself yet. 'I do.'

'Very well. When they come to this dreadful party, I will tell them the truth.'

She feigned affront. 'With me as your party planner there won't be anything dreadful about it. This party will be *superb*.'

One side of his mouth hooked up. '*Sì*, of course.'

He stared at her so long it took a force of will not to hunch her shoulders or snap, 'What?' at him.

'You backed away earlier under false pretences. I'm not searching for relief from a broken heart. But I cannot now help think your actions were wise.'

His words left her feeling hollow and she couldn't work out why when he was merely verbalising her own thoughts.

'I'm not in the right frame of mind to embark on a romantic liaison, no matter how exhilarating it might prove to be. For the next little while, I need the quiet life.' His lips twitched. 'And one thing you no longer are is quiet, Sadie.'

His words surprised a laugh from her. 'True.'

'And, while some flings end well with gratitude and affection on both sides…'

'Some don't,' she finished. 'And we'd rather chop off our right hands than do anything that might strain our relationship with Chelsea.'

His head rocked back. 'If she thought I had taken advantage of you…'

'Or I of you.'

His face grew grim. 'You are very beautiful, but I cannot…'

'Ditto and ditto.'

He leaned across, took her hand and squeezed it, and it felt as if he were squeezing her heart. 'But you are a very good friend, Sadie Beckett. One of the best.'

'Ditto,' she forced past the lump in her throat.

She leaped up, forcing him to release her. 'Now, you'll have to excuse me. I'm going to get changed, and then I have a party to plan.'

But, for the rest of the day, *Enzo thinks I'm beautiful* played over and over in her mind, making it feel as if it were her birthday and Christmas combined.

Sadie was a lark rather than an owl, and Enzo found himself settling into the same patterns and rhythms. He found it oddly soothing.

Her presence could be felt everywhere: in the way Sadie hummed when she worked on the toys; in the way curtains were flung open to let the sun pour in; in the way their movie club competition could make him smile at odd moments. Their last three movies had been *Pretty Woman* for him, *Sabrina* for her and *My Favourite Wife* for him. That last film had so delighted her, he'd felt like king of the world.

Since *Roman Holiday*, he'd been careful only to choose films with happy endings. The lines around her eyes and mouth had started to ease—the comedies were working their magic.

He suspected they were working their magic on him as well. Or was that Sadie herself? All he knew was that, when he was around her, he didn't feel broken any more.

He glanced up at a tap on his office door to find the object of his thoughts standing there.

'Sadie.' He gestured her into the room.

'Am I interrupting?'

A week ago he'd have snapped at her, or muttered something such as, *interrupting is your middle name*, but now he shook his head. 'I'm going over financial records and praying someone will interrupt me.'

'"Interruptions R Us" at your service.' She took a seat and waved a hand at his computer. 'Don't you have people to do that?'

'*Sì.* People more qualified than me, too, but it's good business practice to know what is happening in my own company.'

'Huh.' She blinked. 'So young and yet so wise.'

The admiration in her eyes had him shifting on his seat. 'It's a task that requires concentration and, since the accident and my concussion...'

What on earth...? Why was he telling her this? *Well, as you've told her practically everything else...*

'Oh, I didn't consider that.' She planted elbows on his desk, chin in hands. 'How's it going?'

'As boring as ever.'

His words made her laugh and he found himself grinning.

'What do you have there?' He nodded at the parcel she'd brought with her. She sometimes brought down some treasure from the toy collection to share. He suspected he enjoyed her delight more than the novelty of the items.

'Treasure, of course.' She dimpled at him. 'Is that coffee I smell?'

It was in all the little things—rather than asking if she could help herself to coffee from the pot on the sideboard, she'd not so subtly suggested he get her one. She didn't treat him with kid gloves, she didn't treat him like an invalid and she certainly didn't treat him like an abomination who needed to be endured. Nor did she act as if she was his lackey, which sometimes was the reaction his wealth and success engendered in others—as if those things made him worthy of deference.

His family never did, and he was glad Sadie didn't either. It was a healthy reality check. It was probably part of her overall plan to get him 'party ready'. Rather than resenting it, he found himself appreciating it. He knew she enjoyed cataloguing the toy collection, and he knew she appreciated being away from Australia, but he wished he could help her in a more significant way.

You could ask her about her letter of resignation.

Or he could mind his own business.

He gestured they move to the arm chairs, and he poured their coffees. He set a mug in front of her and took the other chair, trying not to inhale her beguiling fragrance to deeply.

Damn it. Inhale as deeply as you can. You only live once.

As long as inhale was all he did.

Handing him a velvet box, she grinned and wriggled as if she couldn't help it.

He lifted the lid, and inside on a bed of silk

was the pocket watch he'd taken such a fancy to. Lifting it, he once again relished its weight. The gold gleamed beneath the overhead lights.

Opening the cover, his jaw dropped. 'It's working!' He stared at the watch. 'You fixed it!'

She danced in her seat. 'It was tricky and I needed to order some parts in, and I probably should've sent it to someone with more expertise in the area, but yes—it's working again.'

He'd treasure it—even though it was a relic from one of his hideously dastardly forebears.

'It's a beautiful watch, Enzo. Thank you for giving me the chance to work on it. I've also been reading those journals and they've proved enlightening.'

And now she was going to ruin the moment. He set the watch carefully back in its box and braced himself. 'More thieves and tyrants and exploiters of the weak and innocent?'

'Your great-great grandmother did a bit of a potted history of the family. While there was one rather awful landowner that you wouldn't have left your unmarried daughters unchaperoned with…'

He rubbed a hand over his face. 'Let me guess, he was murdered in his sleep?' A fate he no doubt deserved.

'It said he died of the palsy at the age of fifty-two, but his grandfather helped to fund an important university in the region, and not only donated generously to scientific research but also to the arts. The younger grandson, Felix, followed in those same footsteps.

'You also have an ancestor who was part of a diplomatic envoy to Ethiopia. There's a great-aunt who helped found a religious order. Plus there have been numerous civic leaders who've made improvements to their local villages. There's even a couple who were part of the resistance in the Second World War.'

His jaw dropped.

'That Count your father was always so proud of… He actually denied the title before it was fashionable to do any such thing.'

His father had loved bragging about his aristocratic lineage. 'No way!'

'Yes way. The Lombardi name isn't cursed, Enzo. There are some true heroes among your ancestors. It's just unfortunate that your grandfather and father weren't of their number. But, from what I've been reading, your father and grandfather are the exceptions to the rule, not the standard.'

He didn't know what to do with the information.

'So you can use that watch with pride. You're one of the good guys—a hero, not a villain.'

'You've been watching too many romantic comedies.'

She laughed. 'Now, if you really want to get back to your financial reports…'

'I don't.'

'Excellent!' She leapt up. 'Then I want to show you something.'

He found himself on his feet before she'd finished her sentence. A voice in the back of his mind warned him not to look so eager. But, not only had this woman fixed an antique watch he'd had an immediate affinity with, she'd presented him with a different version of his family from the one he'd always held in his mind. One he didn't have to be ashamed of. So, if Sadie wanted to show him something, he'd damn well see it. Not with impatience or bad-tempered grace, but with enthusiasm.

And pleasure, he realised when she dragged him out to the pool house. He'd been banned from venturing anywhere near it for the last week on pain of death. He'd seen the army of delivery drivers arrive over the course of the week, though.

With a flourish, she gave a resounding, 'Ta-da!' and threw open the door.

He headed inside, but stopped mid-stride. *What on earth...?* Sadie had transformed the place!

Rather than crystal and gold-gilt furniture, he was now surrounded by the futuristic furniture of the 1960s. There was an enormous rainbow-patterned bubble-sofa suite, a tan lounger and a selection of chairs in hot shades of tangerine, lemon and lime. Fat cushions in crazy geometrical patterns were strewn about in a riot of brown, orange and avocado. Lava lamps rested on moulded acrylic tables, and disco balls hung where the chandeliers had once been.

He tried to take it all in. 'How did you manage this in a week?'

'I'm a woman of action.' She stuck her nose in the air and pushed her shoulders back, but it thrust her chest in his direction. He stared, his mouth going dry, an instant hunger roaring through him. With a squeak, she immediately slouched again and crossed her arms.

Get a grip. He lowered himself to the nearest plastic banana lounger, pretending to gaze at the room while he focussed on getting the throbbing and fire back under control.

She perched on the edge of a futuristic purple cube that could be used either as a seat or a table. 'What do you think?'

The room. Look at the room.

He did, and when it eventually came back into focus he couldn't get over the transformation. He gazed at the surfboards on the walls, the carnival-style pizza stand at the far end of the room and the jukebox. 'How did you manage all of this in such a short amount of time?'

'Luisa and Guido. They're magicians! They arranged an army of helpers. And one can source anything online these days. And as you'd said money was no object…'

He didn't care what it had cost. This place had been a source of misery to him all his life. But now it looked…*glorious.* He fought an urge to lean across and press his lips to hers in gratitude.

'What do you think?'

His mind raced a hundred miles an hour. 'I think that this party is going to be a great success.'

'Of course it is.'

He even started to believe that he could manage more than the appearance of fun. It struck him in that moment that Sadie was due to return to Australia in a few short days. Every atom rebelled at the thought.

She drummed her feet on the floor. 'I'm going to shake you soon if you don't tell me what you *actually* think.'

'It's just my mind is racing with plans I never thought I'd be contemplating.' He stood and she did too. 'Ten out of ten. I love it, Sadie; I think it is wonderful.'

Her entire body sagged as if his words had melted her. As if his enthusiasm were a superpower. She pressed both hands over her heart, her eyes going misty.

He made a spur-of-the-moment decision. 'Can I ask a favour?'

'Absolutely.'

The generosity of this woman astounded him—it was unhesitating, unstinting. Again, it took all of his strength not to reach across and press his lips to hers. It had nothing to do with gratitude this time, though, and everything to do with dancing hazel eyes, a mischievous mouth and the memory of a long-ago kiss.

Her gaze lowered to his mouth and she moistened her lips. He could've groaned out loud. *Keep things light. Don't go there.*

He dragged his gaze back to her eyes. *Keep them there.* 'Would you consider staying on a little longer and helping me redecorate the castle?'

Her head rocked back. 'I'm not turning your castle into this!' She gestured at the pool house. 'This is great for fun and frivolity, but not for living in up there.' She waved vaguely in the direction of the castle.

'You've performed a miracle. You've made this a place I no longer hate. Not only can I see myself having fun here, I can…' He frowned. 'I could almost imagine a future here.'

A breath whooshed out of her.

'There are rooms in the castle I avoid because they remind me of my father and grandfather. It never occurred to me that it would be possible to erase that and replace it with…' He didn't know what word to use. Hope? Fun?

Comprehension dawned in her eyes. 'With something positive and lovely?'

'Sì.'

Hauling in a breath, he made a snap decision. 'Forgive me, Sadie—I will speak plainly, because I think we can help one another. I accidentally saw your resignation letter when I moved your laptop the other day. Please stay on at the *cas-*

tello, at least until after the party. That's only two weeks away. It will save you having to return. It will also give you a chance to spend some time on new job applications, if that's your plan, while also helping me come up with some decorating ideas. What's more, there'll still be beach time, and a chance to watch all the rom-coms you want.'

She stared at him and he swallowed. 'You're helping me find my feet again, Sadie, and I am not yet ready to let you go.'

CHAPTER TEN

HE'D SAID… SHE…

Don't tackle the man—kiss him!

Which was exactly what she wanted to do. But she needed to rein in her *enthusiasm*. If she was silly enough to do something stupid, like fall in love with Enzo, he'd break her heart. She hadn't been good enough for him nine years ago and that hadn't changed.

She dragged in a breath. Fine; she wouldn't fall in love with him, then. *Simple.* That didn't stop temptation winding around her, though. Taking a step closer, she peered into his face. 'Do you mean that?'

'Yes.'

His eyes glowed with equal measures of defiance and sincerity. She feared she had stars in hers. She *wouldn't* fall in love with him. He *wouldn't* break her heart. At the moment, though, he was helping to heal some of the fractured places inside her. 'Thank you.'

'Don't thank me, Sadie. I'm the one who should

be thanking you. I'm glad you came here to shake up my world.'

He moved a step closer until they were only inches apart. Reaching up, she pressed her hand to his chest. 'I can thank you for being kind, can't I?'

He laid his hand over hers. 'Kind? I was horrible!'

She pressed her hand more firmly against him and a shudder rippled through him. *She* did that to him. *Her.* Air hissed between her teeth as the power and potency of that big male body flooded her senses.

She managed a shrug. 'You were a bit grumpy, but that was understandable. Life has sucked ferociously recently. But, when you found out life hadn't exactly been a bed of roses for me, you were kind, and generous.'

His fingers traced a lazy path from her fingertips to her forearm and she wanted to stretch, purr and…bite him. She swallowed against the raw need that clawed through her. She wanted to sink her teeth gently into his flesh and watch his eyes darken with the same desire that flooded her.

'Why the frown?'

The rasp of his voice lifted the fine hairs on her arms. It took an effort to focus on the conversation rather than the fantasies playing through her mind. 'Your generosity has made me see the lack of generosity in other areas of my life.' She stared at the hand covering hers. 'I've always had to change to win my grandparents' approval—

to not be *too much.* To not be too noisy, to not ask for a birthday party, to not play music or pin posters of boy bands on my bedroom walls. To not demand too much of their energy or time. I've started to see how small I had to make myself.'

Since living on her own, she'd learned to stop living so small. But somewhere along the way she'd forgotten how to dream big. 'I deserve better,' she murmured. She deserved the same generosity from them that she'd given.

His knuckles brushed across her cheek. 'You deserve the very best life has to offer.'

With Enzo, she could be as *much* as she wanted. It was so damn freeing. That didn't mean either the castle or the prince were on offer, though.

Maybe not long-term.

Her gaze lowered to his mouth and she recalled that long-ago kiss. A kiss that had rocked the foundations of her world. She hadn't known a kiss could make her feel, and *want*, so much. She wanted to kiss him again now to find out if she'd imagined it; if she'd somehow exaggerated the power of that kiss in the intervening years.

She nibbled her bottom lip.

A groan left Enzo's throat and his hands went to her shoulders. She thought he meant to put her away from him. Instead those fingers curled around her shoulders as if they didn't want to let her go. 'Don't look at me like that, Sadie.'

The rasp of his voice grazed across all her fine

nerve-endings and she lifted her gaze. The hunger in his eyes emboldened her. 'Why not?'

'Because you want the full, fairy-tale happy ending. You don't want *Roman Holiday*.'

Wait—what?

'I meant what I said the other day. I'm not currently equipped for romance. I'm not looking for love. I don't want the complication or drama that love involves. To be brutally honest, I couldn't think of anything worse.'

And yet he hadn't moved away. '"Forever love" doesn't feature in my future at the moment either, Enzo, if that's what you think I'm looking for.' She frowned up at him. 'My priority is building a new future. Love would be a distraction—a displacement activity.'

She wanted the foundations of her new future to be strong—she wasn't going to rely on anyone else, especially a man, to help her create that. The people she ought to have been able to trust had let her down. From now on she'd rely only on herself.

'Once my life is looking how I want it to, I might turn my mind to love—children might be nice eventually—but at the moment? No.'

His jaw went gratifyingly slack, as if her words had punched the breath from that big body of his.

'I am, however, rethinking my initial reaction to *Roman Holiday*. I'm definitely seeing its appeal.'

The pulse at the base of his jaw pounded. He wanted her with the same intensity she wanted him and she had to fight the impulse to reach up, cover that pulse with her mouth and lathe it with her tongue. 'I'll let you in on a little secret. My life is a bit of a mess at the moment.'

'Not a secret,' he murmured, his gaze raking her face and neck, then down to where her chest rose and fell, leaving a heated path of need in its wake. 'While mine is a total mess.'

'It's not as bad as you think.' She placed both hands on his chest and spread her fingers, feeling the power of his muscles beneath them. Very slowly she ran them up to his shoulders, relishing their width and strength; watching in fascination as his eyes darkened and pupils dilated. 'I don't think either one of us is in the market or headspace for falling in love. Yet I want you and you want me.'

'Sì.'

His nostrils flared. She had a feeling he was drinking in her scent and that thought had her nipples beading to hard, aching points. 'It sounds uncomplicated.' She tried to keep her voice steady. 'We're friends who want benefits, but we also have each other's best interests at heart.'

She didn't want either of them making false promises, but that didn't mean there could be *no* promises. She burned to make love with Enzo, but she didn't want him looking at her with shadowed eyes tomorrow. 'Maybe we need to give each other some assurances first.'

His hands moved to her waist. 'No temper tantrums.'

Her pulse picked up speed. 'Agreed.' She wouldn't throw some Claudia-sized hissy fit—not in a million years. 'We don't let this affect Chelsea.'

'Agreed.'

She stood on her tiptoes until his mouth was in reach. 'Kindness and generosity.'

'Done. But you've forgotten something.' One side of his mouth hooked up. *'Fun.'*

His breath teased her lips and a hot rush of exhilaration filled her veins. 'I can do fun.' She moistened her lips. 'Is it okay if I kiss you now?'

His answer was to claim her lips with his in a lazy, thorough kiss that had her smiling at the relief of it. His hands slid into her hair, holding her still, and his mouth slanted more firmly over hers, his tongue teasing and tantalising, sparking need *everywhere*, melting parts of her that ached for his touch.

Her hands clenched in the material of his T-shirt and she arched against him, seeking relief, revelling in his hardness against her softness. A moan was pulled from the very depths of her. *This*... She wanted *this*.

When he lifted his head long moments later, they were both breathing hard. She hadn't exaggerated that former kiss—not in the slightest. Enzo's kiss was every bit as potent and mind-blowing as she remembered.

Pulling his wallet from his pocket, Enzo extracted a foil-wrapped packet. 'If you'd prefer the comfort of my king-sized bed, Sadie, tell me now.'

Her reply was to turn, walk to the door and lock it. When she turned back round, she slowly made her way towards him, divesting herself of her blouse, bra then her shorts as she went.

His gaze darkened, but when her fingers went to the waistband of her panties he shook his head. 'Let me unwrap the rest of you.'

With unhurried strides he moved towards her, dragging his T-shirt over his head and tossing it off to the side. All that gleaming, manly flesh had her breath hitching. Reaching out, she traced a scar on his chest and another on his bicep. 'Do they hurt?'

He shook his head.

Reaching forward, she traced the scar on his chest with her tongue. He stiffened and groaned, before cupping her breasts in his palms and brushing her taut nipples with his thumbs.

'Oh!' She arched into his touch and he gave her a satisfied smile. The pleasure was so exquisite, it almost hurt. Pressing her hands to his and halting the slow torture of his thumbs, she pushed her breasts against his hands more fully which had another, 'Oh,' choking from her.

'I thought I'd exaggerated the kiss we shared when I was eighteen—made it out to be bigger and better than it could actually have been in reality. But I didn't. You're going to completely undo me, Enzo.'

'And you me. But, Sadie, I promise we'll enjoy every moment. Do you trust me?'

'Yes.'

Their mouths crashed back together and they explored each other with their hands, their mouths and tongues. When Enzo finally rolled a condom onto himself and joined their bodies, they both paused to relish the moment. But then he moved. He'd kept her on the edge of orgasm for so long that after three long, slow, deep strokes her muscles clenched around him. Her body bowed up to meet his, fingers digging into taut buttocks, and she cried out his name as wave upon wave of pleasure crashed, pounded and pulsed inside her, flinging her outside herself to a place she had never been before.

When she finally had the strength to open her eyes, she found him watching her with a strange smile playing across his lips. 'You are beautiful.'

Their lips met in another intensely discombobulating kiss and she felt beautiful. For a tiny moment in time, she finally felt enough for someone, and it felt so damn freeing she wanted to throw her arms wide open to hug the entire world.

Enzo had always made her feel that she was enough. Except for that one time…

But then he did something that made her body quicken for him again. Her eyes flew open to meet his. He grinned, and it was so full of mischief and delight that she couldn't help grinning back. She pushed away that long ago memory. That was in the past. Now, they'd share some uncomplicated fun—soothe and bolster each other until they felt ready to face the world again. She was no longer that silly schoolgirl with stars in her eyes.

Instead you're a grown woman with stars in her eyes.

They're not stars. They're hot, burning embers of passion...

Much later, they lay on the sofa, their hands drifting over each other's bodies—sated, satisfied and probably a bit smug.

Enzo glanced down at her. 'You never got round to answering me. Will you stay a little longer—at least until the party?'

Did he really want her to stay? Now that they'd made love, for him perhaps that itch had been scratched.

He twisted a strand of her hair around his finger and tugged on it gently. 'Let me guess what's going through your mind right now.' That piratical eyebrow lifted and she could've swooned. 'Enzo might be having second thoughts and wishing he hadn't made that rash request...*sì*?'

Was she really that transparent?

'Let me assure you, nothing could be further from the truth.'

She eased away from him a little to settle on

her side. He mimicked her pose, turning to face her fully.

'I meant what I said, Sadie.'

She believed him. Enzo had uttered too many hard truths since she'd arrived at his castle. If he'd changed his mind, he'd have said so. Not in a mean or angry way, but he wouldn't lie about it. He was too tired and still too raw from all that had happened for such lies.

'However, I understand that you may not think staying another fortnight a wise investment of your time.' Lifting her hand, he pressed a kiss to her palm. 'I'm hoping, however, that's not the case.'

Vulnerability stretched through his eyes before it was promptly blinked away. Something in her chest stuttered.

'Did you think I would use and abuse you and then leave?'

'Not abuse, no.'

She wondered if he'd realised that he'd placed her hand over his heart. The slow, steady beats beneath her palm soothed her.

'But you think it's within the realms of possibility that I'd have my wicked way with you and then ride off into the sunset without so much as a backward glance?'

'You don't think that's a possibility? Sadie, I know you are no longer that schoolgirl who had a crush on me, but—'

'I *don't* see you as some kind of trophy, Enzo.

You're not an item I want to tick off some fantasy bucket-list. You're…' How to describe it? She sat up and then wished she had a bedsheet to tuck around her. She felt too naked. 'You're my friend, and you're also an amazing lover. This thing that we're doing…'

Rising, she grabbed his T-shirt and dragged it over her head. He remained stretched out, totally comfortable with his nakedness. Her mouth went dry. Oh Lord; why shouldn't he be? He had the body of a Greek god.

'This thing that we're doing…?' he prompted.

She returned to sit on the side of the sofa. 'I've never had a fling with a friend before—never done the friends-with-benefits thing—so this is all outside of my experience.' She met his gaze. 'But I have a great deal of affection for you.'

His eyes grew wary.

'And I think you feel the same way about me.'

'Sì.'

That wariness deepened and it had an ache throbbing to life inside her. Did he seriously think she'd do some kind of 'Claudia' number on him?

'I feel you have my back, Enzo, and I certainly have yours. I want you to enjoy your party; I want your family to stop worrying about you. And in terms of bucket-list fantasy items—redecorating a castle is right up there. So, yes, I would love to stay. I'd love to do more of…this.'

She gestured to the ridiculous bubble-sofa. 'If that's something you're interested in too.'

* * *

Enzo's wariness drained away. 'That's the part I'm *most* interested in.' He waggled his eyebrows like some pantomime villain, making her laugh. For a moment he'd been worried that she'd declare her undying love for him; would point to the intensity of their love-making as proof of a deeper connection. He could've wept when she hadn't. She'd meant what she'd said about not falling in love.

It didn't change the fact that their love-making had been intense.

That didn't mean anything. They were both going through a lot. It was bound to manifest itself intensely when they found an outlet. But Sadie was right: he wasn't a trophy and neither was she. She was more than an outlet too. She was a true friend. He just needed to make sure they stayed on the right side of the imaginary line they were negotiating.

'I'm glad. Though I feel I'm gaining more from the arrangement than you.'

She gaped at him. 'Summer, castle, Mediterranean, beach, sun…' Her arm gestured wildly in all directions, then her hands dropped to pleat the hem of his shirt. She looked delectable in his shirt. He should encourage her to wear his shirts at every possible opportunity.

Reaching out, he stilled her fingers. 'What is it?'

She wrinkled her nose. 'One of the reasons remaining here is convenient is the fact I have a job interview next week in Rome. So maybe you can also lend me Guido to take me to the train station on top of all of the Mediterranean, sun, beach and castle stuff…?'

He sat up. 'You're applying for jobs in Europe?'

'Yes,' she said in the smallest voice.

If she moved to Europe he might see more of her… He rolled his shoulders. And, that could be nice.

'Do you think I'm being an idiot?' she blurted out.

'What? *No.* Why would I think that?'

'Because it seems an over-dramatic response to me wanting to put some distance between myself and everything that's happened back home.'

When she put it like that…

'But, the thing is, I've kept my life small in lots of ways because of my grandparents. Not that they've asked it of me, so don't think that.'

He had a feeling she'd have loved it if they *had* asked it of her. An ache settled in his chest—a big, purple bruise of an ache. How could they not see what a wonder this woman was and treasure her like she deserved?

'So I've never considered living anywhere other than Melbourne, just in case they ever needed me. Being close at hand seemed the least I could do after they were forced to raise me.'

'They should have taken joy in you, Sadie; treasured having you in their lives, instead of making you feel like a duty.' His hands clenched. 'You shouldn't feel so beholden to them. It is Verity who owes them.'

'I can't help the way I feel.' She shrugged. 'And family can be complicated.'

Huffing out a breath, he nodded.

'What my grandparents care about is having my mother in their lives. They couldn't care less where I live.' She pressed her hands together. 'As much as I wish that were otherwise…' she slid a glance in his direction '…it also frees me up in some rather exciting ways.'

Sadie didn't waste time feeling sorry for herself; she concentrated instead on forging a new plan, a new shape for her life. It shamed him.

'You have a funny expression on your face.' Her brow crinkled. 'Should I be worried?'

He pointed to his face. 'Not a funny expression—*admiration*. For you; I think what you're doing is brave and wonderful.'

If her eyes went any wider, he'd be able to fit a castle, the sea and all of summer inside them. 'Tell me what you most want to do with this freedom of yours.'

'I'd like to see more of the world. To live in a different country for a while and experience life in a brand-new place.' She let out a long breath. 'I want to not be found lacking for once.' She was silent for a moment. 'I want a new start. No baggage.'

He wasn't sure if that last was possible… 'No regrets. Live life to the full?'

A smile spread across her face. 'Exactly.'

'It sounds like an excellent plan. Chelsea will be thrilled that you're moving closer. Tell me about the jobs you're applying for.'

He listened as she outlined the position at the auction house in Rome that she was being interviewed for, and the two jobs in London she'd applied for—one a museum position and the other as a toy restorer at an antiques centre.

She made no mention of starting her own doll hospital. Had she really given up on that dream?

'You've been busy. On top of cataloguing the castle's toy collection, dealing with a grump like me and planning a party, you've been applying for jobs and turning your entire world upside down.'

'Yet there's still been time to amble down to the beach every day to soak up some sea and sun. It's been heaven. And in case you haven't noticed, Enzo, you haven't actually been grumpy recently.'

He blinked. He hadn't just stopped snapping and snarling, he hadn't *felt* like snapping and snarling. He'd continued to put up some token resistance about the party for form's sake, but parties had never been his thing. When he thought of parties, he thought of the extravagant affairs his father had thrown.

He glanced round the pool house. His father would never have thrown a party like the one Sadie had planned. Like Sadie, Enzo could make new memories. If he had the courage.

'Don't make a liar of me now, Enzo.'

Her words were light, but he sensed the concern threaded beneath them. Dragging his gaze back to hers, he sent her a rueful smile. 'Not returning to grump mode. Just trying to trace the evolution of me holding my surliness in check to no longer actually feeling surly.' It had happened without him realising it. That was Sadie's doing.

She shook her head, as if she could read his mind. 'You were already on the mend before I arrived. You've been healing for some time, but I expect it hasn't felt that way. You've been in constant pain for months, but the pain has been easing, yes?'

'I...' He frowned. 'Yes.'

'Look...' she gestured '...you didn't even bring your stick down with you.'

He glanced around, searching for it. Hot damn!

'I don't care who you are; not even Mother Teresa could be cheerful when in constant pain.'

'Sadie, will you please stop downplaying all you've done? I retreated here to come to terms with the accident, but in reality all I did was nurse my sense of injury—and wallow!' *Pathetic.*

She sent him one of those 'school ma'am' looks. 'Stop beating yourself up. You're coming to terms with all of that now, aren't you? So come up with a plan for your life going forward, while doing some fun things like lying on the beach and refurbishing your castle.'

'And having a party?'

'Now you're getting the hang of it.'

Then she yelped and started flinging his clothes at him. 'Luisa is on her way down with lunch!'

Chuckling, he slid into his trunks and chinos while she slipped her capris back on. 'Keep my shirt.'

She wouldn't have time to wrestle with her bra. Reaching down, he picked it up and slipped it into his pocket to save her blushes, though he suspected Luisa wouldn't be fooled for a moment.

Later, over lunch—a delicious chicken pasta salad, crusty bread and sliced fruit—he turned Sadie's suggestion over in his mind. What did he want his life to look like going forward? He had the money to live his life any way he wanted. What did he want to do with all that freedom?

He knew one thing for sure—he wanted to look forward to his future with as much relish as Sadie looked forward to hers.

The next two weeks passed in a haze of golden summer fun that was reminiscent of that long-ago summer holiday Enzo had enjoyed as a boy. He and Sadie walked down to the beach every day to swim, lie in the sun and soak up the serenity. Every day that walk became a little easier.

They pored over ideas for refurbishing the drawing and dining rooms, along with the master bedroom suite. And, in doing so, he started to imagine living at the castle. He could work remotely if he wanted. He didn't have to base himself in Milan and go into the office every day. Even if he did want to go into the office, it was only a two-and-a-half-hour commute. Or he could leave his company in the capable hands of his senior management team and turn his mind to a different project.

Like what?

Ideas turned in his mind. Unlike his father, he'd love to leave a legacy behind that made a lasting impact—a *good* impact.

While this time with Sadie might remind him of that long-ago childhood holiday, there were now some far more adult activities on the agenda. He and Sadie couldn't get enough of one another. With unspoken agreement, he spent the nights in her bed, where they learned the shape of each other's bodies with an intimate detail that utterly delighted him. He loved knowing the spot on her hip that had her melting when he kissed it, and making the air between her teeth whistle when he kissed her nape.

He loved how she could slide a finger down his spine in a manner that made him hard in an instant, and the way she gently sank her teeth into his lower lip in a way that turned him on but also made him smile. And he loved waking up with her warm body curled against his, and loved the way her lips curved into a smile as she woke and blinked sleep from her eyes.

Had a fortnight ever passed more swiftly?

He woke early on the morning of the party

to find Sadie already awake and gazing at him. 'Ready for the onslaught?'

His immediate family was due to arrive early afternoon and would stay for the weekend.

'Not quite yet.' Reaching for her, he kissed her with a hunger that roused an instant and equally fervid response. They made love with a desperate intensity, as if trying to cling to the idyll they'd carved out for themselves.

Nothing had to change, he told himself as he drifted off into a gentle slumber. Once everyone had gone home, Sadie could stay a little longer. She could stay until she found a job.

CHAPTER ELEVEN

THE MOMENT SADIE clapped eyes on Enzo on the landing, she had to clap a hand over her mouth to stifle her laughter. In denim flares and a shirt in an eye-watering psychedelic print—and with the top three buttons undone—he looked as if he had just walked out of Woodstock or off the set of the musical *Hair*. 'You look amazing!'

He struck a pose before flashing a grin that made him look younger. A throb bloomed to life at the centre of her. *That* was how he should always look—young, carefree, *happy*.

Those dark eyes moved over her, his lips turned wolfish and she started to throb in an entirely different way. She'd modelled herself on the movie character Gidget—complete with a Hawaiian shirt, hotpants and her hair pulled into two bunches.

'You look as cute as a button—all sweet and wholesome—and I'm now dying to corrupt you.'

He moved in close and her breath quickened. He hadn't touched her yet, but her every atom had come alive, burning for him. His mouth lowered towards hers. It hovered there, their breaths mingling…

'Lorenzo? Is that you?'

They snapped apart as his mother's voice rose from below. The family had arrived the day before, and they had agreed to meet in the drawing room before walking across together to the pool house. Sadie remained out of sight in the shadows, sagging against the wall, waiting for the strength to return to her legs while Enzo moved downstairs to greet his mother.

She heard their shared laughter, registered their voices retreating in the direction of the drawing room and closed her eyes. That had been close. She and Enzo had agreed to keep their fling a secret. They didn't want the pressure of outside judgements. This thing between them, though temporary, was lovely. And just theirs.

Hauling in a breath, she pushed away from the wall, only for her gaze to connect with Chelsea's, her friend peering over the balustrade from the landing above. Oh, lord, had Chelsea seen…?

She made herself smile. 'Look at you in your mini-dress and GoGo boots. You look amazing!'

Chelsea didn't smile back. Instead she moved downstairs as fast as her pregnancy bump would allow her. 'You're *sleeping* with Enzo?'

Damn it. She met her dearest friend at the bottom of the landing and took her hands. 'Please don't make a big thing about this Chels. We—'

'How can I not? I—'

She pressed a finger to Chelsea's lips. 'Enzo and I are having fun, nothing more. We're both young and…well, in case you've not noticed, I've never really let my hair down.'

Chelsea snorted, as if that was the understatement of the century.

'But I have here, and it's been glorious. It's helped me in ways I couldn't have imagined. And me being here has helped Enzo too.'

Chelsea ignored the latter part of Sadie's statement. 'Helped you how?'

She hesitated. 'He's made me realise I deserve more from my grandparents…and from my life. He's made me realise I shouldn't be settling for second best—that it's not my job to be a consolation prize.'

'I've been telling you that for years!'

'Yeah, but you're biased. And, while I know Enzo and I might be "having some fun"—' she made air quotes '—he's nothing if not brutally honest.'

Chelsea's posture unhitched a fraction and a twinkle lit her blue eyes. 'Well, I have to say, you don't look brutalised.'

Nope, she felt all loved up.

Her friend's eyes turned contemplative then, and Sadie set about shattering that ASAP. 'This thing is temporary; we've both been very upfront about that. We're at points of change in our lives, and just finding a bit of comfort in each other. But that's all this is, Chels.'

'All?' Chelsea didn't look convinced. 'You've always had a soft spot for Enzo.'

Reaching out, Sadie took her friend's hands again. 'I promise not to do anything to hurt your brother.'

'It's not Enzo's heart I'm worried about.'

Chuckling, she slipped her arm through Chelsea's and started them down the next set of stairs. 'I'm a big girl, Chels. There are no schoolgirl crushes here. And guess what? I'm hoping to move to Europe. I've two job interviews next week—both jobs are based in London.'

'No way!'

Chelsea lived in Oxford and, as hoped, the news diverted the conversation into safer channels. Before they entered the drawing room, Sadie eased them to a halt. 'Enzo and I were hoping to keep things secret. We don't want any hullabaloo.'

Chelsea's sigh was audible, but she nodded. 'Your secret is safe with me.'

She squeezed her friend's arm in thanks.

Once assembled, the family moved en masse to the pool house. Exclamations of delight sounded as they took in the 1960s furnishings, the jukebox and pinball machine. Sadie had decorated the individual tables with an assortment of mass-produced toys from the 60s, 70s and 80s, many of which she expected the guests to remember from their own childhoods, all sourced cheaply online.

She grinned as Dominic headed straight for the pinball machine while Stephen pounced on a yo-yo. Isabella lifted a viewfinder to her eyes while Chelsea grabbed a cushion in a crazy geometrical pattern and swung back to Sadie with a silent scream. Sadie asked the wait staff to circle around with glasses of champagne and the first playlist began belting from the jukebox as the other guests started to arrive—an upbeat mix of the Beach Boys and 1960s bubble-gum pop.

The party was a success. Who knew forty people could be so rowdy? There was laughter and dancing; some people swam while others played the games Sadie had spread around—Pick-Up Sticks, Hungry Hippos and even Twister. The pinball machine remained in constant demand.

She'd planned to stay in the background, not draw attention to herself, but Enzo wasn't having any of that. He introduced her to the people she didn't know—not as his party planner, but as his friend. He danced with her and made sure she had something to eat. When she made noises about checking on things behind the scenes, he told her that Luisa and her army of staff had it all well in hand and to enjoy herself instead.

He glared when a cake appeared. 'I didn't know there'd be a cake,' he shot out of the corner of his mouth.

'It's a birthday party.' She kept a smile on her face. 'There was always going to be a cake. That *shouldn't* surprise you.'

'I don't want cake,' he grumbled.

'Then don't eat any. Just blow out the candle and make a pretty speech.'

Which had him huffing out a laugh, before she blended back into the crowd.

He blew out the candle and a rollicking version of *Happy Birthday* rose up around them. He endured it with an odd mix of exasperation and affection, before motioning everyone to be quiet. 'I'd like to thank all of you for coming tonight and making it a celebration to remember.'

He stared into his champagne. 'As you know, this has been something of a turbulent year for me.' His gaze searched the crowd, settling on Sadie. 'But tonight marks a turning point.'

She swore to God her heart performed a triple somersault with a fancy twist. She couldn't have dragged her gaze away from his if her life had depended on it.

'I was initially resistant to the idea of a party, but I'm pleased my resistance was overcome. I want to give a special thanks to Sadie Beckett, who made tonight happen and who transformed the pool house into this vision you see before you.'

Dominic called out, 'Three cheers for Sadie!'

A lump lodged in her throat as the pool house rang with their cheers.

After Enzo's speech, she was swamped with people who wanted to find out where she'd sourced everything, from the furniture to the toys and the caterers. She noted that, as the crowd around Enzo thinned, his mother took his arm and led him out through the French doors to the patio outside.

When the cake had been sliced, Sadie seized two plates to take out to them and had almost reached the door when she heard Isabella say, 'What are you doing, Enzo?'

'What do you mean?'

'You know exactly what I mean. What are you doing with Sadie?'

Her insides scrunched up so tight, it hurt. She immediately turned and walked back into the midst of the rowdy festivities. She had no desire to eavesdrop on Isabella's objections to the situation; no desire to hear rehashed all the reasons Isabella considered her an unsuitable match. Nor did she have any desire to hear Enzo make light of their relationship.

Why not?

She didn't know. Maybe because it would cheapen what had happened between them.

What's to understand? You're having a hot fling, nothing more.

But it felt like so much more. She frowned… and *that* didn't bode well.

'Look what I found on one of the tables!' Chelsea held up a Hawaiian themed Barbie doll dressed in a hula skirt. She crushed the doll to her chest. 'Please tell me I can keep her.'

'She's all yours.' Handing Chelsea one of the plates of cake, Sadie settled with her at a table to catch up on the gossip.

* * *

Sadie blinked when a knock sounded on her bedroom door. She clicked her bedside light on but, before she could slide out of bed and grab her wrap, the door cracked open.

'It's only me.'

Enzo!

'Come in.' She kept her voice low. She hadn't expected to see him tonight. A dizzy rush of delight had her grinning and holding the covers open to him.

He didn't need a second invitation. Closing the door quietly, he moved across the room with a lithe masculine grace, and more than a hint of determination, that made her realise how much his leg had improved during this last month. Sliding in beside her, he waited until she killed the light before pulling her close.

'Tonight was a triumph.'

'Ah, but did you enjoy yourself?'

'The party was wonderful.'

She gave a low laugh. 'It's entirely possible that I embraced my role as party planner with more enthusiasm than necessary.'

A strong hand smoothed the hair from her face with a gentleness that had her eyes prickling. 'Thank you, Sadie, for not giving up on me; for convincing me to go ahead with it all.'

She opened her mouth, but before she could speak he covered it with his own in a warm, reverential kiss that deepened into something so intense, she found herself drowning in the scent, sound and touch of him. Greedy hands tugged at the scraps of clothing in their way, and they joined their bodies in a frenzy of need. She didn't know where that need had come from, but found herself completely incapable of resisting it.

She needed Enzo…*now*. Wrapping her legs around his waist, she drew him as close as she could. She came with a force that shattered her. Enzo swallowed her cries as he too came with a power that left him shuddering in its wake.

They lay there, breathing hard and staring at the ceiling. She turned her head on the pillow to find him frowning. Had that shaken him to the core as well?

She made herself smile. 'Happy birthday, Enzo.'

The frown cleared, his hand finding hers beneath the sheet. 'You're a witch.'

'A good witch, I hope?'

'I like it better when you're wicked. But, *sì*, a good witch. You come here and cast your spells and make everything better.'

She melted to warm toffee. Holding his gaze, she swallowed. 'I hope your mother didn't give you too hard a time.'

His brows shot up. 'You saw…?'

'I was bringing you out cake when I heard her ask you what you were doing with me.'

'Ah.'

'At which point, I turned round and returned to the party.'

He lifted his head from the pillow and mock-glared. 'Why didn't you come and rescue me?'

She stared at him for a long moment. His eyes were bright points in the darkness, reflecting the light from the stars outside the windows. 'I heard her objections after you kissed me nine years ago. I didn't need a repeat performance.'

'You heard…?' He sat up, a frown settling over his face.

With a super-human effort, she kept her voice steady. 'The morning after the ball.'

'She—' He broke off. 'Tell me exactly what you heard back then.'

She sat up too. She didn't want to make a big song and dance about it. It *was* nine years ago. 'Only her say it had to stop. *It* being us.'

'And then?'

The weight of his stare burned through her, but she couldn't lift her head to meet it. 'She said, "Sadie is not from our world. She doesn't have the resources to negotiate the world you come from".'

Isabella had witnessed their kiss and her disapproval had sliced right through Sadie's soul. *Sadie is not from our world...* Those words had tormented her ever since. Once again, she'd been found wanting. Once again, she hadn't been enough.

'Oh, Sadie.' Enzo pulled her into his arms.

She couldn't resist the warmth or the proffered comfort, but she didn't want to hear his rationalisations or explanations. 'It was a long time ago. It doesn't matter now.'

'Of course it matters. I wish you'd eavesdropped a little longer. Then you'd have heard what she was really worried about—that you were too young. She was worried my father and grandfather would eat you alive: those were her exact words. And she was right—they'd have been unforgivably awful. Not just rude, but spiteful. They'd have sought out your vulnerabilities and played on them. She said you deserved to be treated better than that, especially as you were so young.'

'Hold on.' She eased away. 'She was *worried* about me?'

'You see, she'd had to put up with their ugliness for so long. She didn't want to see another young woman victimised. Especially not one she was fond of.'

Her jaw dropped. Isabella *hadn't* thought her deficient and not good enough. She'd wanted to *protect* her.

'She was also worried I was toying with you and would break your heart. She told me, if I did that, I'd be no better than my father.'

Ouch! That would've hit him hard.

'She made me see the rift I could cause in the family if I did hurt you—Chelsea would never have forgiven me.'

Sadie slumped against the pillows.

'She never disapproved of you, Sadie. Not then and not now. Once again, she's worried I will hurt you.'

Reaching out, she took his hand. 'That's not going to happen. I know you're not interested in falling in love. But, just so you know, your sister witnessed our near-kiss on the landing.'

He rolled his eyes ceilingward. 'Of course she did. What did you tell her?'

'Kept it light. Said we were both just having some fun—promised not to break your heart.'

'Which is pretty much what I told my mother.'

'Then I told her I was moving to Europe and that moved the conversation on.'

He sent her a sidelong glance. 'I told my mother you'd performed a miracle—that you'd turned me from someone who was cranky and snarly into someone fit for company again.'

'You *didn't*!'

'I did.'

That shouldn't make her so happy. 'I told Chelsea you'd made me realise I was worth more than the scraps my grandparents tossed to me.'

'*So* much more.' His nostrils flared. 'I also told my mother you've made me feel strong again.'

He felt strong again…

She tried not to grin too widely; tried to shrug insouciantly. 'I did tell Chelsea we were brutally honest with each other.'

'I should've mentioned that too.'

Moonlight lit the room and she could see the way his pupils dilated and contracted. He cupped her face. 'You're beautiful.'

He made her feel beautiful. 'I hope you're not tired, because I'm sending you what I'm hoping is my wicked witch, seductive smile.'

'It's working,' he growled. And then he kissed her.

Afterwards, Sadie lay awake for a long time, staring up at the ceiling, a horrible suspicion starting to take hold. This had started to mean too much to her: Enzo telling her how wonderful she was; how she deserved the very best life had to offer. Her heart gave a sick kick. Was she in danger of falling in love with him?

A frigid chill slid between her ribs. She *couldn't* do that. He'd made it clear love didn't feature in his future—*very clear. That* wasn't going to change. She needed to pull back. Her pulse started to hammer. She couldn't repeat the same soul-destroying patterns that she had with her grandparents. She couldn't.

Right. She needed to focus on the future. She needed to get ready to embark on that future. Her tenure at the castle was temporary. It was time to stop putting Enzo's needs ahead of her own and choose an end date.

None of those assurances made her pulse slow. She hadn't fallen in love with Enzo. She *hadn't…*

From a long way away, a voice sounded through her: *liar.*

* * *

The party, and the weekend spent in the company of his family, lightened something inside Enzo. But it didn't stop him from breathing a sigh of relief when they finally left. Things could now go back to normal with Sadie and him.

There shouldn't be *a normal with Sadie. There shouldn't be a normal with any woman.*

Claudia had laid bare something that had been crystallizing in his mind for some time. The women he dated were mostly cold and calculating, but he never discovered that until it was too late. Why could he not see through their disguises? He was no longer prepared to deal with the tantrums, the fits of pique, the sulking, or the outbursts. He would *not* turn his life into the same kind of battleground that his parents' marriage had been.

He'd always been a solitary creature. The thought of living alone didn't cause him any particular pangs. But Sadie had made him see that he could enjoy a fling—especially when the boundaries were agreed upon at the outset. Besides, Sadie wasn't just *any* woman. She was a friend.

Something had changed since the party, though. She'd become… Quieter wasn't the right word, nor was reserved, but he'd catch her biting her lip and staring off into the distance, a frown on her face. The moment he said her name, she'd shake herself and send him one of those big, mischievous smiles, but they no longer had the ability to put his world to rights. And he didn't know why.

'Did someone say something to you at the party?' he finally demanded. 'Or over the weekend?' *Heaven forbid.*

'Like what?'

'Something to upset you.'

That snapped her to attention. 'What? *No.* Enzo, your nearest and dearest are good people. Why would you think any of them would say something mean to me?'

'I said plenty of mean things to you when you first arrived, but I'm still a good guy.'

She eyed him up and down and gave a careless shrug. 'You're alright, I suppose.'

Which had him barking out a laugh, before scowling. 'You're not considering going back to Australia to abide by your grandparents' conditions?'

Her chin hitched up so fast, it should've given her whiplash. 'Absolutely not!'

He let out a breath.

'I hope they'll eventually see they can have a relationship with me that's separate from Verity, but I'm not going back to beg for whatever scraps they'd feel duty-bound to offer me if I did agree to toe their line.'

Reaching out, she took his hand. 'You've shown me that I'm worth more than that.' A funny expression flitted across her face, but it was gone again in an instant. 'I'm sorry if I've been preoccupied. I've been thinking about these job interviews I have coming up.'

She had two online interviews this coming week. If they went well, she'd progress to in-person interviews in London. Waiting on the threshold for a new life to begin had to be exciting, but probably nerve-wracking too. Her preoccupation made sense, yet that didn't stop a kernel of unease unfurling inside him.

At night, though, they made love with an intensity that infused him with joy. And something less intense but somehow deeper—*contentment*. A month ago he could never have foreseen this, could never have imagined it. He felt as if he'd been handed a miracle, and he wanted to pay tribute to that miracle.

'I've made a decision about my future,' he said.

They were down at the beach and Sadie's head spun round with flattering speed. 'What kind of decision?'

They lay on their towels, drying off after a swim, and the sand shifted obligingly beneath him as he turned to his side and propped his head on his hand. 'About what I'd like to do going forward.'

She was stretched out on her tummy, wearing a red bikini that he itched to peel from her body. She peered over the top of her sunglasses at him. 'Don't keep me in suspense.'

'I have all of this.' He gestured around. 'A castle, extraordinary grounds and a beautiful beach. It's too much for one person.'

She sat up, giving him her full attention. 'And?'

'I've been making enquiries—talking to people in the know—and I'm going to open it up during the summer for disadvantaged children to come and have a holiday.'

Her jaw dropped. She pulled off her sunglasses, her eyes wide. A lump lodged in his throat when he recognised the emotion reflected there: *admiration*. 'What an utterly perfect thing to do.'

He did his best to swallow the lump.

'To give a child the chance of a once-in-a-lifetime holiday—like the one you had when you were ten…'

And like the one she'd given him this summer.

She clasped her hands beneath her chin. 'To make something so positive from this place… What's the saying—making a silk purse from a sow's ear?'

He started to laugh—a simple chuckle that grew until he fell back on his towel, gripped with huge belly laughs. Eventually he sat up again and met her bemused grin. 'Sadie, in nobody's language can a castle ever be considered a pig's ear.'

'Pfft.' She waved that away. 'I'm glad you're not going to sell all of this to some cold-eyed tycoon who'd fill it with expensively hideous things simply to prove how successful he is.'

A man like his father? No. Instead Enzo would leave behind him a legacy he could be proud of. He'd reshape the future of the castle using his earlier forebears' examples—the ancestors Sadie had told him about. He'd never have known about them if she hadn't done her digging.

'It's an incredibly generous thing to do.' Sadie reached across to briefly clasp his arm. Before he could place his hand over hers, though, she removed it. It shouldn't have given him pause—she'd been leaning at a funny angle—and yet he couldn't shake off a sense of unease.

He tried to shrug it away. 'I have all of this through an accident of birth. It feels right to share it.'

'I don't doubt that you'll enjoy every moment of this new venture of yours.'

He suspected she was right. 'If you hadn't reminded me that I had the means to live my life in whatever fashion I wanted, I'd have probably returned to work in Milan and continued making a lot of money developing property.'

It was not that he wasn't proud of his company; he'd worked hard to make it a success, though it was naïve to believe he'd not had help. He'd had a trust fund, his family name and an excellent education. His father might've been a miserable excuse of a man, but Enzo had been gifted all the advantages to ensure he could make a financial success of his life.

'But it would've been mindless.' And his company deserved better. So did he.

'You're ready for a new challenge now.'

'Sì.'

'I wish you every success with your new venture, Enzo.'

She said the words as if she was saying goodbye and things inside him tightened. 'Will you come and visit when I have my first contingent of holidaymakers?'

'Of course!' But her smile was worryingly bright.

His heart thumped. 'Have you made some decisions about your own life too?'

'I…'

'Come,' he said when she hesitated. 'I've told you about mine.'

'What?' Her lips curved into a mischievous grin. 'Like an "I'll show you mine if you show me yours" thing?'

That smile, the twinkle and her teasing, made everything okay again. 'Absolutely.'

'But I feel as if we should wallow for a little longer in your plans. Imagine the children laughing and running on the beach, the sound of their feet pounding up the stairs in the castle, the way they're going to saturate the pool house with their shenanigans.'

He gave a mock groan. 'There will be water fights, will there not?'

'Bound to be.' She rested back on her towel and placed her sunglasses back on her nose. 'I'm seeing cream teas on the lawn… There has to be cake—lots of cake—and games of cricket.'

'Cricket is a game I do not understand. Football, however…'

'Football followed by gelato.'

Perfetto. 'And movie nights.' He'd enjoyed his and Sadie's mini comedy festival.

'And bedtime stories.'

He stared at her, but her eyes remained hidden behind her sunglasses. 'Bedtime stories?'

'Yeah. Didn't your mother read you bedtime stories when you were little?'

She had, and he'd loved it. He settled back down. Sadie hadn't had bedtime stories, birthday parties or hugs and laughter. His chest burned. 'It will be idyllic. I will make it one of the best times they have ever had. A memory to hold close.'

'Just as you have for me.'

Glancing across, he found a smile curving her lips. Reaching out, he took her hand and squeezed it. What a gift this woman was.

She squeezed it back, and he told himself that nothing was different; that all was still right with the world…

Enzo led Sadie out to the terrace and removed his hands from her eyes. 'Okay, now you can look.'

She opened them and her mouth formed a perfect 'O'. 'Ooh, Enzo! This looks utterly wicked.'

'When you mentioned cream teas on the lawn, I realised how remiss I'd been. Not once had I offered you a decadent afternoon tea on the terrace.'

She kinked an eyebrow at him. 'I promise you,

the one thing I haven't been during my stay is hungry.'

The words were uttered with a wicked twinkle that made him grin. He held out her chair, poured the tea and served her a huge slice of cream cake. She took a bite and moaned in appreciation. '*So* good.'

'I feel as if I'm redeeming myself.' He tucked into his own slice of cake. 'And I am also hoping to now worm from you your plans for the future, after having wallowed so comprehensively in mine all morning.'

'Ah.' She set her fork down and reached for her tea. He couldn't help feeling she was fortifying herself. 'I'm pleased to report that I have face-to-face interviews for both positions that I applied for in London.'

'This is not a shock. You're wonderful, and any employer would be lucky to have you.'

She twinkled at him, but something about it had him frowning. 'On the spur of the moment, I also applied for a job I thought I'd have no chance of—a position as a researcher on an antiques-restoration TV show—and I have an interview for that one now too. My fingers and toes are crossed!'

'This is excellent news!' A cloud passed over the sun, though—metaphorically speaking, as there wasn't a cloud in the sky. If she was offered one of these positions, their time here would come to an end.

Still, it would be several weeks before she would start a new job. They could relish what time they had left. 'I'll organise us flights to and from London.'

She shook her head very slowly. 'I've loved every moment of my time here, Enzo, but it's time for me to stop my dillydallying and finally embark on this new life of mine.'

Dillydallying? He blinked. Was that all he'd been to her—a dalliance?

It was what you agreed. It's what you wanted.

He nodded, frowning. It was.

Have you changed your mind?

The memory of his parents' constant fights rose in his mind. His heart gave a sick kick as he recalled how Claudia had lashed out at him. He ground his teeth together. *No!* He wasn't going to put himself through any of that again.

CHAPTER TWELVE

'NEVERTHELESS, THERE'S NO need for you to make any hasty decisions, Sadie.'

Sadie nearly choked on her cake. The one thing she hadn't expected was for Enzo to encourage her to stay longer. She'd already over-stayed her visit by an extra three weeks. She thought he'd be…well, not exactly delighted; while she'd tried to create some distance between them during the day, she'd been powerless to do so at night. Nights continue to be tangled limbs, breathy sighs, sweaty bodies and ecstasy, followed by a deep and profound peace when Enzo wrapped her in his arms as she drifted off to sleep.

So, while she hadn't expected her news to delight him, she'd thought a big part of him would be relieved. She couldn't read the expression in his eyes. 'What makes you think my decision is hasty?'

He gestured at her cake, encouraging her to continue eating, but thoughts of leaving here, of leaving Enzo, had her appetite fleeing. It had become starkly clear to her over the last few days that her attempts to emotionally distance herself from Enzo were doomed to failure. She'd fallen in love with him—utterly, completely and *pointlessly* head-over-heels in love with him.

She needed to leave. Staying here would be self-defeating. He didn't want love in his life. Wishing and hoping otherwise wouldn't change that. She deserved more. She deserved better. Enzo himself had pointed that out on more than one occasion.

'You've not yet attended these interviews. You don't know if you will be offered a position.'

Her hands and jaw clenched. Did he think she wasn't good enough?

'Sadie!' He snapped out her name and she glanced up to find him glaring. 'I expect you will be offered *all* of these positions. I also think, until you decide which job you want, it makes sense to base yourself here. When you know where you're going to work, you can then find a place to rent.' His brow pleated. 'Does this not make sense to you too? This way, you will only be moving once.'

As she'd only brought two suitcases with her, moving wouldn't be a problem.

'And if you stay longer…' He sent her one of those slow grins that turned her knees to wet spaghetti. 'We can continue to enjoy the sun and beach, among other things.'

And that was the problem. She'd been enjoying it all too much. Enzo had come to mean *too* much. And she was now in a bind of her own making. 'You and I have always been brutally honest with one another, yes?'

He frowned. 'Are you going to be brutal now?'

She laughed. 'I promise I'm not.' She wasn't even going to be honest, though he didn't need to know that. 'Enzo, I've started enjoying all of this too much.'

His frown deepened. 'What do you mean?'

'We promised to keep things fun and light and drama-free.'

'Is this not what we have done?'

On the surface, perhaps, but things had also been unexpectedly hot and heavy. It had taken her off-guard. She didn't even have the heart to berate herself for falling in love with him. In hindsight, it seemed utterly inevitable. She'd loved her time here; loved her time with him. She refused to regret any of it. But she could no longer hide from the fact that pain loomed in her future—a lot of it—and to remain here any longer would only hurt her more.

If Enzo had taught her one thing, it was that she deserved better—that she should never settle for being second best. She deserved more than the few scraps of affection he was currently capable of giving.

'Sadie, is that not what we've done?' His voice sharpened. 'Dear God, please tell me… Have you…? You haven't developed *feelings* for me?'

Lifting her chin, she shook her head, proud

of herself for not wincing at his horror. 'No.' It was a bald-faced lie, but she'd promised him she wouldn't fall in love with him. She'd promised him to keep things drama-free. She might've broken that first promise, but hell would freeze over before she broke the second.

'No, Enzo, but we also promised to keep things temporary, and I fear that if I stay much longer I'll develop more permanent feelings for you.'

She met his horrified gaze—his beautiful, horrified gaze—and her heart pounded so hard, it hurt. 'Now, if that's something you're interested in exploring…'

He shot away from their little table so fast, she felt as if something vital had been physically torn from her chest. With all her heart, she wished she could laugh at the expression of horror plastered across his face, but she couldn't. Not when her heart lay at her feet in a million tiny shards.

The pain starts now.

She dug up a smile from somewhere. *Keep it drama-free.* 'That's a no, then.'

'Sadie…'

'There's nothing to apologise for, Enzo. This holiday has been every good thing—a ten out of ten. But I think it wise for me to pack my bags and leave in the morning. And don't worry—we'll keep in touch. I can't wait to let you know which job I choose, if I get them, and where I end up calling home. Next time you're in London, we'll catch up over dinner or something, yes?'

'Yes.' The word croaked out of him, and it was all she could do not to drop her head to her hands.

'In the meantime, I'm going to finish my cake.' She shovelled cake into her mouth, feigned a moan and sent him a thumbs-up, gesturing that he too should finish his cake. She'd read somewhere that people comfort-ate because the physical act of eating helped reduce stress.

Not working...

But, look at her, keeping things drama-free. *Go me!*

He took his seat again, sending her a funny look—half-wary, half-unconvinced. 'We need to go back to being friends without benefits *immediately*!' He stabbed a finger onto the table.

A dastardly part of her couldn't resist teasing him. 'What? You think I'm going to fall head over heels in love with you in the—' she glanced at her watch '—next sixteen hours?'

He rolled his shoulders. 'Of course not! I just...'

'Chill, Enzo. No drama, remember? We promised.'

His mouth worked. 'Are you accusing me of being dramatic?'

She waved her fork through the air. 'If the cap fits...'

She finally finished her cake. *Thank you, God.* 'Look, everything is fine. We go back to being friends, no harm done.' She set her fork down on her plate. 'It's no big deal, is it?'

'None at all,' he managed through gritted teeth, though he didn't finish his cake.

'We should have a final film night, though—with popcorn,' she added, in case there was something to the comfort-eating hypothesis. She grinned. 'And I have the perfect movie for us.'

Roman Holiday!

Enzo glared down the long drive as Sadie's car disappeared. He'd offered to take her to the airport himself—had almost insisted—but she'd rejected the idea so completely, he'd let it drop.

He growled. He should've insisted.

Maybe it's easier for her this way.

That was the reason he'd refrained from insisting. He'd do anything to spare her pain.

She said she hasn't developed feelings for you.

Yet, when he'd made it clear he had zero interest in pursuing anything longer term, she hadn't been able to hide the flare of pain in her eyes.

Confronted with the same horror, wouldn't your feelings have been hurt?

Damn it. He should've been kinder. He should've said something gallant: *if there's anyone who could make me change my mind, it's you.* He should've said something to make her laugh and accuse him of flattery. But he hadn't, and his reaction had made her feel bad about herself. He'd give anything now to go back and change that, do better.

Despite her assurance otherwise, had she developed feelings for him? Had he inadvertently hurt her? And, if he had, how could he fix it?

You can't.

Then how could he lessen the damage?

Another growl emerged from deep in his throat. *He couldn't.* The best he could do was stay away and hope she hadn't been lying—hope she hadn't developed feelings for him. He didn't want to stay away, though. He wanted to check on her. If he didn't, who else would?

She doesn't want you checking on her.

Which made him growl again.

Damn it! Last night she'd made him watch *Roman Holiday* again. Now he couldn't get the damn movie out of his head. What on earth had he been thinking, giving it ten out of ten? He'd give it a big, fat zero now.

Turning on his heel, he set off for the kitchen. He needed strong coffee and something sweet, such as a slice of Luisa's panettone.

He halted in the doorway when he found Luisa standing at the bench, wiping tears from her cheeks. '*Mio dio!* What is the matter?'

She glanced around with a start.

'Sorry. I did not mean to startle you.'

She waved that away. 'Your Miss Sadie left me a gift.'

She wasn't *his*.

'And a thank-you note…' She reached for a pretty card with an image of a mug of steaming coffee and a big slice of cake on the front. 'For feeding her "such splendidly and utterly delectable treats". As if it's not my job and what I'm paid to do.'

'You went above and beyond—serving all of her favourite things. You made her feel special, and I appreciate it, Luisa.' She'd been wonderful, as had Guido. The other man had willingly put himself at Sadie's beck and call, always happy to help her move some heavy object or other in the attics.

Luisa held up a pair of pretty opal earrings and a sheet of folded paper. 'She left me her favourite pavlova recipe and told me it would have Mr Stephen swooning.'

'I will look forward to sampling it as well.'

'I shall miss her.'

'Yes.'

The castle seemed oddly empty without her. He might miss her, but their affair had always had an end date. Perhaps that end date had come sooner than he'd anticipated, but it was what they'd agreed. He had no intention of changing the rules to explore something deeper with her. Too many women in the past had turned from warm and charming into angry balls of rage when he couldn't be what they wanted. He wasn't sure he'd be able to stand it if Sadie were to turn on him like that. It would be safer to keep his distance and ensure that never happened.

He helped himself to coffee from the pot.

'Can I get you anything else, Enzo? Biscotti…?'

'No, thank you.' His stomach had gone too hard and tight for food.

Taking his coffee upstairs, he strode into the drawing room, but had no idea what to do there. He turned round, headed for his office instead and sat at his desk. He didn't turn on his computer, though. Instead, he stared at the wall opposite. His coffee went cold.

An hour later, he shot to his feet and strode back through to the drawing room, glaring at the table sitting beneath the bay windows. It seemed wrong that Sadie no longer sat there, tinkering away with some toy or other, her clever fingers working their magic and bringing the toy back to life.

Like she brought you back to life?

Sì. Her presence had dragged him out of the doldrums.

Are you going to fall back into them now?

Absolutely not!

He lifted his gaze to the view. The beach! *That* was what he'd do. He'd go and sit on the beach and swim a little, as he and Sadie had done. Just because she was no longer here didn't mean he couldn't still enjoy the routine they'd created.

Forty minutes later, he found it impossible to wipe the scowl from his face. The beach had lost its magic. Without Sadie, the sun didn't shine so brightly, and the water wasn't as invigorating. Even the sand felt lumpy and hard.

'Rain, damn it,' he muttered, staring at the

cloudless blue sky. Rain would suit his mood more than this summer perfection.

When he retired for the night, he found a little parcel on his bed. His heart picked up speed. Inside were the clockwork figures he and Sadie had restored—the twirling ballerina and the flamingo. The accompanying card read:

Put these where you'll see them every day, to remind you to be playful, to have fun. Life is for living (to the full!), Enzo, but it's also for chasing one's dreams. I'll never forget my time at the castle. Sadie xx

Enzo spent the next three days trying to come up with a different routine—one that didn't remind him of Sadie. He swam laps in the pool first thing every morning. He spent his days working on his 'summer at the castle' project—getting two national charities onboard and finding qualified people to administer the programme. He spent the evenings in the drawing room reading the journals Sadie had brought down from the attic. But, while the routine was different, she was always on his mind.

And he spent far too much time winding up those clockwork figures and watching them twirl and dip. During the day, he kept them on her table in the drawing room where he could see them. He took them up to his bedroom when he retired for the night. He wound them up and watched them until they ran down and then wound them up again. It was while he was in the act of reaching for the twirling lady on the fourth morning without Sadie that the truth finally hit him.

He thumped down into the nearest chair, staring out of the bay windows to the lights glittering on the water below. He'd spent so long worrying about Sadie's feelings and Sadie's heart that he hadn't stopped to examine his own. All this aching and yearning…

His mouth went dry. He missed her. He missed her in a way he'd never missed another soul before in his life. With every fibre of his being, he wanted her here with him.

His mind raced and so did his heart.

He *loved* her.

He sat with that for a long moment. The women he'd dated in the past had lied about who they were; they'd hidden their schemes and greed behind charming veneers. Sadie hadn't tried to be charming. Not once.

Leaping to his feet, he seized the clockwork figures before moving across to his DVD library. Grabbing a bag, he dropped selected DVDs into it and then raced upstairs to grab his passport.

Sadie might not have feelings for him, but she'd indicated she'd be open to exploring and deepening their fling into something more. In letting her go so easily, he might've lost his chance with her, but there was only one way to find out. And he wasn't going to let her go without a fight.

'Yay!' Sadie mumbled, leaning against the wall of the lift as it whooshed her down to the foyer of the fancy London high-rise where she'd had her interview. *They'd love to offer me a position with the company.* Her shoulders slumped. *Great.*

She ought to be jumping with joy. Instead, she scowled as the lift doors opened to let her out into the grand foyer that was all marble and glass, and reminded her of the pool house back at Enzo's castle. She'd thought when she'd been driven away from the castle that she'd be able to compartmentalise her pain—put it in a box marked 'Enzo' and somehow keep it separate from her new life. She trudged across the foyer. What a joke! Missing Enzo overshadowed everything.

She walked about in a fog, as if a dark cloud had descended over her—one that not only refused to let the light in, but threatened to suffocate her—which made it impossible to feel happy about something as trivial as a job offer.

You still have to eat. You still have to pay the rent.

'Shut up,' she muttered.

'The interview didn't go well, then?'

She slammed to a halt and fixed her glare on the man in front of her. A man who looked a lot like Enzo. She saw Enzo *everywhere*. Usually it was some broad-shouldered, dark-haired Adonis moving through the crowd ahead of her, whom logically she knew wasn't Enzo. But it never stopped her pulse from racing or hope from gripping her heart.

Reaching out, she pinched his arm.

'Ouch,' he said mildly, a piratical brow lifting.

She started. Oh, God! It really was… '*Enzo!* What are you doing here?'

'Why did you pinch me?'

'Just making sure you were real.'

A slow grin hooked up one side of his mouth. Her heart started to thud. In her grey fog, had she given herself away? It was all she could do to not stamp a foot in frustration. She'd worked so hard to save face during her last day at the castle. To blow it now…

She hitched up her chin. 'And, in answer to your question, the interview went very well, thank you.'

Hold on. He was *smiling.* If she'd given herself away, he'd be running as fast as he could in the other direction.

'So that pinch…' He ignored her statement about the interview. 'Are you saying you've missed me?'

She didn't have the resources for light, flirtatious banter—not this week. She folded her arms. 'What are you doing here, Enzo?'

Something in his face gentled, and he reached out as if to touch her cheek, but pulled his hand back at the last moment. 'I came here to tell you that I love you.'

She blinked and leaned towards him. 'I beg your pardon?'

'I...'

A crowd of people exited the lifts, accidentally jostling them. Taking her arm, Enzo led her across to the bench that ran along one wall where people could set up work stations or simply sit and watch the busy street outside.

Had he said...?

Surely not?

He settled her on a stool and then opened his briefcase. Pulling out a package, he unwrapped it to reveal the vintage clockwork toys she'd left for him. 'I'm in danger of wearing these out. I spend most of my nights winding them up and watching them again and again—hours on end. I watch them in an effort to try and recapture the fun and magic of when you were at the castle.'

A lump lodged in her throat.

'I went into a panic when I thought I might've hurt you. I couldn't think of anything worse. It drove me out of my mind.'

The lump promptly deflated. Her gaze dropped to her hands. 'That's guilt, Enzo, not love.' She didn't want his guilt and regret. She didn't want those things tarnishing the happy memories they'd shared.

'Which is what I thought too. Until I realised

I was hiding behind that, too scared to face the truth.'

Her heart started to pound too hard and too fast, despite her warnings for it to do nothing of the sort.

'The truth is that I love you, Sadie. You taught me to embrace life again. You showed me how glorious that could be.'

Her hands twisted together. What she wouldn't give for his words to be true… But *that* was gratitude. And she didn't want his gratitude any more than she wanted his guilt.

'But when you left, I felt in a worse place than I had been before your arrival.'

She stiffened.

'And yet in a better place too, because you'd helped me dream a new dream and I still had it, even if I didn't have you.'

The lump surged back into her throat.

'That dream is worthy, and I mean to see it through, but I've lost my enthusiasm for it. And you want to know why? Because you're not there to share it with. My life now feels like it's fifty percent less because I don't have your dreams to cheer for. I want your dreams in my life, Sadie. I want to celebrate your successes and be there when—' he gestured to the lift '—things don't go to plan.'

'I was offered the job.' Her voice sounded as if it came from a long way away. 'I've been offered all three jobs I applied for.'

'Then why aren't you happy?'

She raised her eyebrows, letting them speak for her.

He gave a decisive nod. 'I love you, Sadie, though clearly I have yet to convince you.' He suddenly scowled. 'And, just so you know, the ending to *Roman Holiday* is terrible. I can't believe you made me watch it again. It's a dreadful movie.'

'It's a brilliant film!'

He waved a finger beneath her nose. 'Our love story does not have to end in that way.' Seizing his briefcase, he pulled out a stack of DVDs. '*My Fair Lady*, *Pretty Woman*, *Ever After*, *Notting Hill*.'

As he said their names, he pushed each DVD into her hands. She stared at them. These were all Cinderella stories. Was he asking her to be his Cinderella? Her heart pounded, fit to burst.

'You indicated you'd be open to deepening our relationship. Please tell me that's still the case. Our love story can end like these ones if only you'll give me the chance to prove that to you.'

If only she'd give him the chance… Did he mean it?

Her heart lodged in her throat and pounded there. 'You were adamant you didn't want love in your life. You swore that you didn't have the resources to deal with the drama a relationship involved.'

Taking the stack of DVDs from her, he set them

on the bench and perched on a stool, pulling it closer so that his knees bracketed hers. Reaching down, he took her hands. 'All my life I've been confused about what love looks like. My mother claimed to love my father—but all I saw was bitter arguments and fights and my mother crying.'

She squeezed his hands. She couldn't help it.

'And then Claudia claimed to love me, but lashed out in such a physical way…and with such terrible consequences.'

Acid burned her stomach. Claudia's actions could've killed him.

'It has made me equate love with turbulence and fury and upheaval. I did not want any of that in my life.'

She didn't want any of that for him either.

'But then you came to the castle with all of your sunshine and smiles and teasing.' He frowned. 'And, when we argued I was the dramatic one, not you, you didn't throw temper tantrums. When you considered yourself in the wrong, you apologised.'

'So did you.'

He stared at his hands. 'My mother might've loved my father, but he didn't love her. He didn't treat her with respect. He flaunted his lovers; that's what their arguments were about. My father wasn't capable of loving anyone but himself. You, though, do respect me.'

'Yes.'

'As for Claudia… Hers was the temper tantrum of someone too used to getting their own way, not the act of someone who loved me. *You* do not throw temper tantrums.'

Her throat thickened and she had to swallow.

'And then you made me watch romantic comedies and…'

She leaned towards him. 'And?'

'Those movies demonstrate characters becoming *better* people because of love, not worse. They might behave badly during the course of the movie, but then they find the courage to change and make whatever sacrifices are necessary to win their loved one's heart.'

The words he uttered made beautiful and logical sense… But could she trust them? Could she trust *him*?

'I've realised that the women I've dated in the past—women I thought were charming and lovely—were lying about who they were and putting on a performance. They were hiding their true selves behind pretty veneers. But you don't do that.'

'No.'

'I didn't believe anyone could bring out the best in me, but you did. I'm a better man for having you in my life. The question now is…do I bring out the best in you?'

Of course he did.

'And can you face your fears for me?'

She stiffened. 'What fears?'

'That you're not good enough. That you don't belong in my world.'

Her face grew uncomfortably hot.

'You ran, Sadie, rather than tell me the truth. You ran. You didn't stay and fight for me—for us.'

'I promised I wouldn't fall in love with you. And I promised there'd be no drama. I did *not* promise you honesty.' She moistened her lips. 'I didn't mean to break the first promise, so I did everything I could to keep the second one. When I checked to see if you were open to taking things further…'

'I shut down.'

'You didn't just shut down, Enzo, you looked sick with horror, and I didn't want to be the cause of so much distress. Confessing my love wouldn't have brought you joy. It would've brought the exact opposite. And I figured you'd been through enough.'

'Confessing your love…?' He touched a hand to her cheek. 'You really love me, then?'

She stared into that beautiful face, those steady eyes, and the dark cloud surrounding her slowly evaporated. Enzo *loved* her. Not only did he love her, not only did he think her enough, he thought her *extraordinary.*

A smile stretched across her face until she thought she'd become all smile and nothing else. An answering grin stretched across Enzo's. Slipping off her stool, she moved into the circle of his arms, looping her arms around his shoulders.

'I love you, Enzo. I can't promise you a drama-free life. But I can promise to walk that drama beside you.'

His hands settled on her waist and he pulled her closer. 'If you're beside me, I won't even notice the drama.'

Oh, Lord, this man could melt her to a puddle with his words and the heat in his eyes. Reaching forward, she covered his lips with hers and kissed him with all her heart—with all her hope and love. He kissed her back with an intensity that stole her breath.

When they eased apart, they were both breathing hard. His eyes glittered. 'Where's your hotel?'

'Not far.'

'*Dio!* We need to go shopping first. I brought nothing with me except…' He gestured to his briefcase. 'And I'm not leaving you now. Not even for a day to collect my things from the castle.'

She wanted to float up to the ceiling, happy dance and kiss him again. 'You're not afraid I'll run away again, are you? I promise not to do any such thing.' She leaned against him, relishing the strength of that big, masculine body. 'Instead, I'm going to make your life so full of fun and laughter and love, you're going to have to pinch yourself to keep making sure it's real.'

Enzo smiled down at her. 'I do not think you're going to run. But as one of the heroes in one of those movies said—when you realise what you want your life to be, you want to start that life as soon as possible. My life feels as if it has started today. And I am not going anywhere.'

She simply stared, letting the magic of his words wash over her.

'Now, how does this sound? I can work remotely, so when you decide which of the jobs you want to accept, we'll buy a place of our own. One you will love and…'

She pressed her fingers against his mouth. 'We already have a home we love. You always knew what I most wanted to do—to set up my own doll hospital. With your help, I could do that.'

It was time to stop being so afraid.

His eyes glowed. 'I love you, Sadie. I'm yours—heart and soul.'

'That's a nice line,' she whispered.

'I've been practising.'

His smile filled her vision. 'Take me home, Enzo.'

'That's a better line,' he said, before kissing her with a fierceness that made her toes curl.

Lifting his head, he took her hand in his. 'Let's go home.'

* * * * *

If you enjoyed this story, check out these other great reads from Michelle Douglas

Tempted by Her Best Friend Billionaire
The Venice Reunion Arrangement
Secret Fling with the Billionaire
Tempted by Her Greek Island Bodyguard

All available now!

The VISCOUNT'S FORBIDDEN FLIRTATION
Sarah Rodi
A GOVERNESS to REDEEM HIM
Lottie R. James
FREE
Value Over
$25

Faking It with the Boss
Another Shot at Forever